After Christmas, Martina wakes to a world of trouble. How can she run her café when her staff is MIA? Who is that handsome gooseman at the market? Why does he crash her café with six geese? *Gott im Himmel!* Where is the gentleman lover of her dreams?

The staff have left a message on a Christmas napkin. If it means what Martina fears, a family row is brewing.

Dequan's plans to spend Christmas with his cousin are thwarted when Lucy gets a better offer. Now he's at a fairy-tale B&B.

The people seem nice but peculiar. Six geese seem — oddly homicidal. Are they really chasing Dequan, or is it his Christmas feather they're after? What's with all the eggs? Then, at the market, he sees the *fräulein* of his dreams.

After taking refuge in *Fee Kaffee*, Dequan fills in for Martina's missing staff, but the geese are still on his case and laying eggs.

Martina has a feather bed that's big enough for two. Dequan's mystery holiday takes a delicious turn — until the geese, the café staff and his phone bring reality crashing in. It's such a mess, and Martina needs a holiday.

Geese a Laying
Copyright © 2020 Lark Westerly
ISBN: 978-1-4874-3170-9
Cover art by Martine Jardin

Published by eXtasy Books Inc or
Devine Destinies, an imprint of eXtasy Books Inc

Look for us online at:
www.eXtasybooks.com or www.devinedestinies.com

Geese a Laying
A Fairy in the Bed

By

Lark Westerly

DEDICATION

For my ever-patient editor, Amber, who helps to disentangle my italics.

AUTHOR'S NOTE

The *Fairy in the Bed* series features a sprawling cast of characters who wander in and out of one another's stories. For more about this series, visit Lark's website at https://larksinger.weebly.com

Geese a Laying comes under the category of the 2020 Twelve Days of Christmas set. It is part of the *A Fairy in the Bed* series. It stands alone, but you may recognise some of the characters and settings.

Martina Bless appeared in *Sunshower,* and also in the *Counterpoint* books. Dequan Qin had a small but pivotal role in *Queen of the May.* The story of Lili, Chiara and Yannick is told in *Just Eloped.*

Linda and the folk at the B&B all appear in multiple books.

Like *Queen of the May, Geese a Laying* and its companion, *Just Eloped,* are largely set in 2020. When I wrote *QotM,* Covid19 wasn't even thought of. By the time it was published, we were in the middle of a pandemic. Since it was far too late to rewrite the story, I had to let it be. My philosophy is that as the world of *Fairy in the Bed* is not *quite* our world, we can accept that in that reality the pandemic didn't happen in 2020.

For more information on the *Fairy in the Bed* series and the related *Red Cat, Tamzin* and *Pixie Grip* series, please check out Lark's homepage at https://larksinger.weebly.com

Here you'll find character lists, glossaries, a timeline and other information.

CHAPTER ONE: GENTLEMAN OF THE BEDCHAMBER

Martina Bless, Patterdale, Victoria, December Twenty-seventh

Martina watched the feather drift from the carved canopy above her bed to land, soundlessly and almost intangibly, on her curvaceous naked body.

A Christmas angel must be flitting by.

It tickled her left nipple, and Martina blinked.

Not very angelic.

She put up a hand to brush it off, but it flitted away to tease her lips.

Oh, it's you, my gentleman!

Martina smiled as a joyful certainty ran through her body from chin to toes. She opened her arms and lay waiting rapturously for the next touch of the feather.

Her gentleman of the bedchamber. That was the way she thought of the loving, playful presence that sometimes came to her just before she slept. She had no idea who he was or what he was. She didn't think of him during the busy hours at the café. He never intruded on the rare times she took a lover, but, oddly, she didn't notice his absence until she was alone and he came again.

"Not to be dictatorial, *meine Liebe*, but could you give me something more substantial than a feather?" She stretched and added, laughing, "Not that it is my place to order the universe, but a woman needs a full-fledged man, and it helps if he's visible."

She reached out in hope, but the feather danced away.

"Tangible would be nice. The feather's fun, but can't you give me a lovely cock to play with? And arms to hold me?" she said.

The feather, white and larger than a hen's, returned to her nipple, painting it with shivers of delight.

Martina gasped, and her body convulsed in shudders. She cried out in a loud yodel and then collapsed in the downy support of her goose feather bed.

When she had her breathing under control, she said, with a hint of reproach, "I know you'll leave me now, but couldn't you let me keep the memory this time? No? Well, give me a sign, at least. Waking up alone is getting a bit . . ."

The feather, which had been spiralling gently in the moonlight, floated down to land on her chest.

Martina put her hand over it, finding it soft to touch, with a firm quill. She lifted it to her lips and kissed it.

"*Danke, meine Liebe. I wish I could have had you for Christmas. Oh, and some conversation would be nice. Maybe we might wake up together on New Year's Eve?*"

She tucked the feather under her pile of pillows. When the universe gave you a sign, it made sense to put it somewhere safe.

A cuckoo sang out. Martina snapped awake. She glanced at the wooden clock that ticked up the hours in her bedroom—five o'clock. It was much too early to open the café, though Yannick would be out there doing the baking, dourly thumping dough.

She wondered what he thought about during those solitary hours when the kitchen of *Fee Kaffee* belonged to him.

The Christmas rush was over and New Year's Eve wasn't for a few more days. The casual staff had dispersed. Lili and Chiara would soon be—Martina's thought broke off there.

She sat up in her pin-tucked nightgown. Hadn't she just

been naked with a feather tickling her nipple?

What?

She swung her legs out of bed and pulled down her counterpane. She'd finished it just before Christmas Day, having devoted half an hour of every evening to her patient stitching. It was bright and delightful, from the cosy partridge cuddling a pear in his wings to the twelve drummers, whom she'd based on musicians she knew. She'd enjoyed the challenge, although she'd made only seventy-eight of the figures rather than the more ambitious total of three-hundred-and-sixty-four.

It was a generous spread. It needed to be, to cover the bulky feather mattress.

She went to splash her face in her small bathroom before dressing for the day. She brushed out her light brown hair and braided it. Her fingers fumbled with haste.

Hurry, hurry . . .

No hurry. It's early, remember?

Remember.

Remember what?

She forced herself to slow down as she ate her usual breakfast of rye bread and coffee in the chalet kitchen before she went to the market with a basket on each arm.

Martina stepped out into the dawn-lit garden, where tables and chairs formed the outdoor portion of the café. She hesitated to call it a beer garden. That sounded rowdy, and rowdy was something she was not.

It was warm already, and she headed out through the gate into the square and along two streets to the open-air market where the merchants of Patterdale traded fresh produce.

Most of the stallholders were human, and she greeted the ones she knew with a smile. Some of them were aware she was an alpenfee, but they all accepted her as part of the Patterdale community. Her family, the Blesses, had lived on the human side of the gates ever since her four-times-great-uncle

Marti Bless married a human woman and agreed to *live human* with her back in the nineteenth century. His twin brother, Kettil, already wed to an alpenfee *mädchen*, crossed to the human realm as well. *Living human* was a matter of interpretation, which the twins' descendants adjusted to suit themselves.

"Given the girls a holiday, Ms Bless?" one young man asked, interrupting her thoughts.

"No, why do you ask?"

He looked disconcerted. "Usually they get the salad things for the café."

"Today, my lad, you must content yourself with me," Martina said.

Even in the soft early light, she saw him flush.

"Sorry. I didn't mean it that way. Always happy to serve you, Ms Bless."

Martina pulled herself up. She was being *formidable* again, as her younger brother Dario liked to say. "No, *I'm* sorry. You're quite right. Usually, it *is* the twins' job to do the marketing. I woke early, so I thought I'd save them the trouble."

That wasn't quite right, but she wasn't about to babble to a nice young human man about the odd urges and premonitions she thought of as *the sight*. Lots of alpenfee had it, but it was unpredictable, and, this man was human.

"Good Christmas?" she asked.

"I ate too much. Great-uncle Gus set fire to the Christmas pudding and swallowed the sixpence," he said.

Martina laughed, hoping it was a joke.

He handed her bunched baby carrots and freshly pulled lettuce. "Got some nice radishes and a good big cucumber, if you need them."

"I'm sure you have," she said dryly.

"Tell Lili and Chiara the party starts at six," he said.

"I will."

She wondered about that party and which of her twin

nieces he favoured.

He won't get either of them. He's a nice lad, but Nina would have him for breakfast.

She moved on to the next stall.

"Lili coming in later?" the tomato seller asked, piling perfect romas into a bag.

"No—" Martina heard the uncertainty in her voice and stopped suddenly.

What am I doing here? Marketing is the girls' job, not mine.

Oh, well.

By six-thirty, she had what she needed—time to return to the café.

Lili and Chiara would be there by seven, so she had time to tell them the marketing was done, unless they elected to go straight to the market. She might end up with double-of-everything—

Better conjure them a note. Or—

Again, she lost her train of thought.

They're not going to come.

Nonsense.

When she first opened *Fee Kaffee* three years ago, it made sense to hire her twin nieces, who were seventeen and, as they informed her in chorus, *done with school.* She hadn't expected them to stay long, but they were still with her, neat, quick and indefatigable. The patrons loved them. Her baker, Yannick, grumbled at them but then, he grumbled at everyone, including Martina. They responded by addressing him as *little brother* because he was a day younger than Chiara who, by dint of being born at five minutes after midnight, was technically a day younger than Lili.

The twins never missed a shift, although she hired casuals sometimes. Casuals had all covered the pre-Christmas rush. They wouldn't be in today.

Neither would Lili and Chiara.

Why would I think that?

Why do I know that?

Her thoughts were interrupted by a raucous honking and she turned to watch the incongruous sight of a tall man striding through the market pursued by a small flock of geese.

"*Gott im Himmel!*" Martina said aloud. She tended to lapse into alpenfee dialect in moments of astonishment. The twins did it, too, which annoyed their mother.

The gooseman was tall, with a slightly rumpled appearance. He had a clever, expressive face that puzzled her. He looked . . . *different*. Maybe he was one of the more eclectic blends of fay or one of the rare kanaalfee. That would account for the unusual face structure.

A man taking his geese to market wouldn't have surprised her *over there* in the fay homeland. It looked odd in the human realm. She'd heard of folk leading pigs with a bucket of apples, but geese? What was he up to on this side of the gates? If he intended to *pass*, he was doing a poor job of it. She was drawn to go and ask him.

I'll enquire about goose eggs to make eierbrot. *That will give me an excuse.*

She was heading after him when someone touched her shoulder.

"Greet ye, Martina! Twins not here?"

Martina turned away from the puzzling gooseman and focused on Cèilidh Acushla, who lived *over there* but who came through the gate to work at the *Pride of Erin*.

"I'm doing the marketing myself." For once, she didn't ask after her friend's complicated family. Cèilidh had leprechaun blood, and leppies always wanted to answer family questions with precise regard to who was related to whom, and how.

Cèilidh flashed her dimples and said, "Road rise to ye, darlin' Martina. I hope the blessed saint brought ye a gift for your bed?"

"Not yet," Martina said.

"A wish on it, darlin'?"

"Why not?" she said, laughing.

"So what is it to be?"

"You choose for me."

"Indeed. I'll send something your way." Cèilidh went on in a swirl of green skirts.

Martina looked for the handsome gooseman. He had disappeared.

Had he been there, or was he just a picture conjured by *the sight*?

Why did I think of goose eggs? If I went home with those, Yannick would look at me and ask since when do we make eierbrot outside of Easter? Not that he'd say it aloud, but I'd hear what he was thinking.

The baskets were full, so she ducked between stalls, where she was screened from human gaze. She conjured the marketing to the café for Yannick to deal with.

He'd be grumpy about that, but at least he'd be spared the twins' brand of double-decker conversation. They loved provoking Yannick. She ought to tell them to stop.

But not today.

They weren't coming in to work today.

She was sure, but she had no idea why.

CHAPTER TWO: MESSAGE ON A NAPKIN

Martina Bless, Patterdale, Victoria, December Twenty-seventh

In her bedroom, Martina leaned in and breathed on the pier glass. Her reflection fogged, and she concentrated, picturing the twins. *The sight* came when it pleased, but sometimes it was possible to encourage it.

The glass swam with mist. Instead of her nieces' rosy faces, she saw a white feather.

What in the world?

The feather faded, but the brief vision sent her across to her bed on a flash of memory. She lifted the pillows.

No feather.

Her heart jolted with disappointment.

Seriously, Martina? You did know the gentleman is a dream, right? Even while you were dreaming him, you knew. You weren't really expecting some gentleman to stroll in to light up your life?

She dumped the pillows on the bed.

Her mobile rang.

Martina snapped her fingers and it popped into her hand.

Nina.

Nina was the twins' mother, married to Martina's brother, Florien. Nina had degrees in medical science, and she thought her girls were wasting their lives by working for Martina.

Florien, caught uneasily between his strong-willed wife and his determined daughters, had said, "Let's call it a gap year. They can earn some money and learn how the world works. They'll soon see they need some qualifications."

Nina and Martina both knew the twins, having shaken the ink of academia from their brains, would prefer an income to further study.

"They'll learn management and customer relations skills from me," Martina had said.

"In a café."

"Yes, Nina, in a café. People have to eat."

Nina thought people should eat frugally at home. She said so, often. Did she intend to be insulting, or was she blind to the implications of what she said?

Martina thumbed *accept*.

"*Guten morgen, schwester aus Liebe,*" she said.

"Martina?"

Who else would answer my phone and call you sister-by-love? She bit her tongue to keep the words back and said instead, "What can I do for you, Nina?"

"Where are my girls?"

Martina glanced at the cuckoo clock. "Not here yet, unless they're in the kitchen."

"Check, will you?"

Nina sounded exasperated, so Martina hurried downstairs and unlocked the door between her cottage and the café. "Yannick? Are the girls in yet?" she called.

She thought her taciturn baker would at least favour her with a grunt. She paid him well for his cooking skills, not for a sparkling personality. His skewed body clock made him somewhat nocturnal.

"Yannick?"

She stepped through. There was no enticing smell of fresh bread. The dough pans were empty. The marketing remained in the baskets.

She went into the connected garage where Yannick Langel parked his van when he arrived at three in the morning to begin the day's baking.

9

It wasn't there. Neither were the twins' bicycles. Only her seldom-used hatchback sulked against the inner wall.

Martina huffed.

He's not coming either.

The phone quacked as Nina insisted on an answer.

Martina wanted to thumb *end call,* but provoking Nina was unwise.

"They're not here, Nina." She didn't say they wouldn't be coming. Nina didn't believe in *the sight.*

"Have them call immediately when they arrive," Nina said. She broke the connection.

"*Guten morgen* to you, too," Martina muttered.

She loaded the woodfired oven. The bread should have been on hours ago. Too late now. It would have to be *eierbrot.* This was alpenfee egg-bread. It was nominally an Easter dish, but it was quick to make.

I should have got some goose eggs from that handsome gooseman.

She could try to call the twins. What was the point? Nina would have tried already, and Yannick rarely answered his phone.

She went to the larder where, to her surprise, she found the ingredients laid out ready for the egg-bread. A large white feather curved around one of the eggs. They weren't the traditional goose eggs, but they would have to do.

Martina stuck the feather in her pocket. She dumped strong rye flour in an industrial-sized basin, made a well, poured in buttermilk and beer and got cracking. Yannick, or someone, had lined the egg bowl with a linen napkin printed with Christmas symbols. When Martina took it out to wash the bowl, she found it bore a neatly inked two-word message in its white centre.

Just Eloped. It was enclosed in a heart.

The twins.

"*Gott im Himmell!* Nina is going to kill me," Martina said.

CHAPTER THREE: SPAG TOM WITH LUCY

Dequan Qin, Sydney, NSW, December Twenty-third

Four days before Martina saw the gooseman at Patterdale market and found a perplexing message on a napkin, Dequan Qin was on the Manly Ferry, leaving another satisfied client in his wake.

The harbour sparkled in the December sunlight. Dequan was texting his cousin.

Lucy-Lou – Ping!

He'd sent that one every day for the past week.

Today there was a response.

Ping yrself

Dequan's heart lifted. His Lucy was back in the land of phones and television and catch-ups over coffee. Lucy was his best friend, his little sister, his moral compass, his wavelength twin and his go-to-gal for a hug with no misunderstandings. She got him. She always had. The trust between them was such that when she'd asked him to find her a nice man to teach her the ropes in bed and to make sure those ropes never turned into strings he'd done as she asked without question. He'd also provided her reliable car.

Lucy garaged the car at Gran Qin's house whenever she was away. Grandad took it out once a week to keep the battery alive.

She'd walked away from the no-strings lover, though. For a couple of years afterwards, Otto Fairling had asked wistfully after Lucy whenever he encountered Dequan. These days, he was married — sort of — to two women, neither of whom was Lucy.

Spag tom tonite? Lucy pinged back.

In the pan!

Pasta with homemade tomato sauce and fresh bread was a ritual whenever Lucy was in Sydney. He had the tomatoes already. Lucy's green-fingered friend Nelis had brought them round the day before.

Yum

He took a deep breath. *Got something 2 run by U*

K. C U 7 xxx

Three kisses? She must be feeling expansive.

Dequan pocketed his phone.

Lucy.

His cousin spent months each year working on an offshore island with no phone reception and no computers. She was meant to have time off in May, but if she had, she must have spent it elsewhere. He hadn't seen her in months.

Two hours later, he heard her key in the door.

"Come in, Lucy-Lou!"

Lucy had *carte blanche* to come in whenever she needed a roof, a meal, a chat, or a shoulder. His girlfriends didn't agree on much, but they all thought the Dequan Qin and Lucy Tan dynamic was weird and unacceptable.

He'd broken up with Puck in mid-December and he wondered whether he'd subconsciously been clearing the decks for Christmas with Lucy.

Footsteps approached. "No *klompen at the gates*, I see."

"Not at present." It was another ritual. His mother had given him a pair of clogs in one of her *remember your heritage* moments. Whenever he had a girlfriend in, he'd park them at the door as a warning to knock before entering.

He pushed the tomato sauce off the stove and shook the pasta. Then he turned to greet his cousin.

"Lu—good God!" He was so startled he dropped the colander.

Lucy tsked and bent with less than her customary grace to rescue it. Unlike Dequan, who was tall and blond like his Dutch-Australian mother, Lucy was a pocket-sized person who looked like their mostly Chinese grandmother. She was also—

"Good God!" His world rocked on its axis.

Lucy straightened, holding the colander. "Lucky this landed right side up. Even on the island, we don't trust the five-second rule." She thrust the colander at him. "Serve up. I'm hungry."

Speechlessly, he took the handles.

Lucy snapped her fingers. "Get with the program, Dequan." Her face creased in a delighted grin, and she held out her arms. "Come here, you great lunk."

He dumped the pasta into bowls and bent to give her a hug. "You're pregnant?"

Lucy got up on tiptoe to kiss him. "No! Am I really? I hadn't noticed!" She stood back and broke into a peal of laughter. "Your face!"

Dequan said cautiously, "Do Uncle Adam and Aunt Cherie know?"

"Not yet. Gran Qin does. I went straight to her when I got off the ship last night. I was done in, and I had to pick up the car. Anyway . . ." She lifted back her long black hair. "It's wonderful to see you, Deq."

"Likewise. Er—"

Lucy spooned tomato sauce over the pasta and picked up a bowl. "You said you had something to run by me?"

Dequan motioned her to the breakfast bar. "I'll tell you after dinner."

She dug her fork into the mound of pasta. "Yum. I've been hanging out for this. We don't make spag tom on the island.

No idea why." She ate hungrily and mopped up the sauce with a piece of bread. "So?"

Dequan pushed his bowl aside. "It's about Christmas."

"You're going to your parents, aren't you? Since you're between *klompen* gal-pals?"

"Not this year. Mum's found a new cousin from the Dutch side of the family windmill. She's called Marieke, and she lives on a tulip farm in Tasmania. Mum and Dad are sailing down on a yacht with Marieke's son and his family."

"Gran Qin will give you Christmas dinner."

He said, "I have a better idea. You remember that mystery holiday voucher from Vouch-Safe?"

She nodded.

"I tried to use it after I broke up with Puck. I got all ready to go, but the driver said it wasn't valid."

"Puck?"

"My immediate ex. She's Dutch."

"Sounds like a Shakespearean fairy. Would I like her?"

"Yes. She's lovely. Calm, kind and patient."

"Why is she ex-*klompen* then? You deserve lovely. It sounds as if she deserves you."

He shrugged. "Why did you dump *darling Otto*?"

"That's a low blow. You know he was strictly catch and release."

"Sorry."

"So am I." She smiled. "Forget it. Why was the voucher *not valid*? You know I work for one of their subsidiaries, and I've never heard of a voucher being invalid."

"The driver said it was for two people, and I'd need a second traveller. She said now it was activated in the system, it would expire on New Year's Eve."

"Ask an ex-*klompen* gal-pal. Ask lovely Puck. You're still on speaking terms?"

"Of course."

"That's my Dequan. Never crap in the nest you might want to come back to." She snagged a bunch of grapes from the fruit bowl.

He said, "Ma and Dad will be tiptoeing in the tulips, so I thought you and I could use the voucher for a Christmas break. We could leave on Boxing Day. Unless you have other plans." He kept his gaze on her face.

Lucy said, "Hmm."

"I take it you do."

"I do. They involve lying under a hawthorn tree with my divine Paris and fucking like bunnies."

Dequan blinked.

"You could come with me. I'm sure you could find someone to do while I'm doing Paris. You'd have to find your own hawthorn tree, though. Paris wouldn't care if you shared ours, but I'm peculiar that way."

"*Lucy. WTF?*"

Her smile deepened, and her eyes narrowed like a sleepy cat's. "Sorry, Deq. I'm a bit punch drunk and a bit scared. I love you like a brother, but I want to be with Paris."

"Paris! And you thought Puck was an odd name?"

"Not now I know it's Dutch. Paris is—" She stopped, giving a curiously private smile.

"Do you feel like telling me about him—about that?" He indicated her bump.

"Okay. You know what I do on Ferris Island, right?"

"You act as a camp companion. No names, no tech, no pack drill, no fraternisation. Well, I thought that was the deal."

"Exactly. Campers or camp companions with pre-existing relationships can fraternise, but only with one another. I met Paris on the island in April. We slid through on a technicality because we met before the camp began. That gave us the pre-existing relationship that meant we could legitimately fraternise."

"So you did. Fraternise, I mean."

"Not much just at first. We spent a few days at the camp in uncomfortable celibacy. Then things got complicated. He—Paris—took me *over there* to sort ourselves out. After that, I got to meet his mum."

"*Over there*," Dequan repeated.

"*Over there*. Fairyland—not. Where Gran Qin used to take us when we were kids."

"Oh. There." Dequan seldom thought about those childhood visits to the place Gran Qin insisted wasn't really called *Fairyland*. Being a little bit fairy through a distant ancestor wasn't something he explained to most people. He was half Dutch and almost half Chinese, and that mix was a big enough stretch. If he mentioned his courtfolk great-great-something, the human friends would look blank. Any fairy friends might pity him for being so far *down the line* as to be barely even a trace fay.

Lucy rapped her knuckles on the breakfast bar to get his attention. "Dequan!"

"Hm?"

"*Over there*." She pointed at him and moved her finger a few times, presumably to make sure he was tracking. "*Over there* is where Paris lives when he's not on the island with me. It's where *I'm* going to live part of the time when I'm not on the island with him or duty-visiting Mum and Dad and the Grands." She sighed deeply. "My life is perfect, but I don't know how I'm going to manage Mum about *this*." She jerked a thumb at her bump.

Dequan said, "You don't have to manage her, technically. You're twenty-seven. You don't live with Aunt Cherie. She'll have to know, but there won't be anything to *manage*."

Lucy drew a circle on the breakfast bar with her forefinger. "I know, but I'm her only child. My children will be her only grandchildren. I don't feel right about taking that away from her. She does love me, even though she disapproves of my life choices. Besides, Paris and I think our children should know their whole heritage. He lived with his mum, but Jack — his dad — has always spent lots of time with them. Jack's dad visits, too."

"You can bring your kids to Sydney."

"That mightn't be possible. Paris is a waterfolk halfling, and the air in Sydney makes him feel ill, though he's okay on the island. That means Mayflower might not thrive in a city either." She patted her bump.

Dequan tried to get his head around the fact that Lucy was expecting a part-fairy baby who might never be able to live in the human world.

"Lucy-Lou, the ball's in your parents' court. If they want to know their grandchild, and if you're right and she . . . or he — "

"She, so Paris says," Lucy put in.

"If she can't come to them, then they'll have to go to her. Can Aunt Cherie open the gates to *over there*? Dad can't. Even Gran probably can't do it now."

"You know how Mum is about fairies. She doesn't want to know. Paris's dad uses the gateway in Glebe, so I expect he'll pilot them if they agree."

"Sorted. Tell your parents they can visit you any time. They *should* have the chance to know their grandchild. I know Mum regrets never knowing her Amsterdam grandparents. That's why she's digging up Dutch cousins on the *Bloodline* site."

Lucy sighed. "You're right. It has to be their decision, and I will accept it and not let it bother me. Will you come with me to break the news?"

"Sure, as long as you make it very clear very quickly that I'm not responsible for — er — Mayflower."

Lucy's eyes creased in another grin. "God, yes. That would be the last straw."

"Why doesn't Aunt Cherie like me?"

Lucy sighed. "She thinks I love you and Gran and Grandad more than I love her."

"Is she right?"

"Yes. You and Gran have always embraced what we are. Mum has spent a lifetime trying to deny it."

"Blood will out," Dequan said.

"Indeed. A little drop of fairy blood goes a long way if you let it. I *did* consider the consequences before Paris and I made Mayflower. We even discussed it with Jack and Fee—that's Paris's mum. Paris said he wouldn't mind if I made a child with someone else, but you know my philosophy."

"*I'm going to have it all,*" he said, deadpan.

"Yes. I want Paris. I want to work on Ferris Island. I want you as my best friend. I wanted Mayflower to be made with Paris and not some random human man. You should have seen Paris light up when I asked him to *make a babby.* He loves children. All waterfolk do."

"I rate a mention in your catalogue of wants?"

"You always will. Paris understands that. Mind you, he's the only lover who could understand you and me. Except for darling Otto."

Whom you left.

Dequan got up to make coffee and said, in the most neutral voice he could manage, "You'll be spending Christmas with Paris, then, rather than Vouch-Safe Mystery touring with me?"

"Yes. You would be welcome to come *over there,* too. I mean that sincerely. Paris will love you because I love you."

"I'll pass on that, Lucy-Lou. Can't let that voucher go to waste."

Lucy said, "If you'd asked me last year I'd have said yes like a shot. Tell you what, though, I can get the company to exchange it for a single one."

"Can you do that?"

"I have shares in V-S, so I get shareholder perks. I can do that right now. I'll have the confirmation sent to your phone." She clicked her fingers. "Gimme. I'll sort it, and you can trip off alone as soon as you like. That do?"

He brightened. "That would be great. I'd hate to waste it by letting it expire or taking a *klompen* pal just for the sake of it."

"Any preferences? Weekend? Week? Tropics? Snow? Active? Lazy?"

He shook his head. "I'll leave it up to Vouch-Safe and the universe."

"Excellent. I'll do that, and then you can come to Mum and Dad's with me. If the shit hits the fan and they throw me out, I'll stay the night with Gran."

"And after that?" he said, hoping for one more day of Lucy's time.

Lucy hugged herself. "I'm seeing Nelis and Xavier for breakfast, and in the afternoon I have a date with Paris under a hawthorn tree."

She keyed an address into his phone. "Date of travel?"

"Boxing Day."

No use waiting if Lucy's not going to be here.

"Done."

Dequan held out his hand for his phone, but Lucy retained it. "If you're coming with me to defuse Mum and Dad, you'd better change that shirt."

"What's wrong with it?"

"It has a big tomato stain down the side. There's also a hole in the pocket." Lucy stepped up and wiggled her finger through the hole to demonstrate. There was a faint tearing sound as the threads gave way. "The luck will drain through that, along with stray five-cent pieces."

"Really?"

She extricated her finger from the hole. "Could be. Take it off and I'll give it the coup de grace. Don't worry. I'll do it with gentle respect."

He looked down at himself, seeing his shirt through her eyes. "It's my favourite thing. It's so comfortable."

"That's because it's been washed almost to cobwebs. You can find another favourite thing if you open yourself to the possibility. All things must pass."

He perceived she wasn't talking about his shirt.

Sadly, he pulled it off and handed it to Lucy.

Riiiiiipppp! The sound of the coup de grace was no more than a whisper, as if the shirt had indeed been made of cobweb.

Chapter Four: Goose Feather

Dequan Qin, Sydney, December Twenty-fifth

Two days before Martina saw the gooseman at the Patterdale market and found her staff missing in action, Dequan Qin ate Christmas dinner with his grandparents and with Lucy's parents.

Lunch was long on holly and tinsel, but noticeably short on Christmas cheer. Cherie Tan was affronted and inclined to blame Dequan. This was unfair. It wasn't as if he'd encouraged Lucy to make a baby with a fairy man who couldn't live in the human realm.

Mind, Dequan wouldn't have discouraged her either. Why shouldn't she take whatever nice things the universe chose to offer? She was doing no harm to anyone, except, indirectly, to those of her family who were trying to enjoy their Christmas dinner while Cherie was affronted.

Not Lucy's fault. Maybe not Cherie's, either.

Gran Qin proposed taking the Christmas lunch to eat as a picnic *over there* with Lucy and her lover. That seemed sensible to Dequan, but no one else looked enthusiastic. He wished his parents were there. Lotte would have been all for it.

After dinner, Gran Qin cornered Dequan in the kitchen and gave him a gift.

She did that now and then, and the gifts were always bizarre. He kept them in a glass-fronted cabinet in his flat.

Today's gift was a white feather mounted on a gold pin.

"Are you implying I'm a coward, Gran?" he asked.

She did her best impression of an enigmatic walnut. She wasn't all old, but she could look old if she wanted. "Of course not, darling. Why would you think that?"

"Didn't people give white feathers to conscientious objectors?"

"Maybe, but this is a keepsake my great-grandfather gave me just before he died. And don't get the wrong idea. *I'm* not dying for a long time yet."

"That's good. Was this great-grandfather the courtfolk man?"

"That's him. The last pure fairy in the family tree. He was old when I was born, but my father used to take me to visit."

"What was his name?" Dequan asked.

"I don't really know. I called him *Great-Grand-Pere.*"

"And he gave you a feather."

"He said it was from a fay goose." Her eyes swivelled towards Cherie, who was ostentatiously clearing the table. "My children had no interest in such things, but you need this."

"Gran Qin, I have no idea what you're talking about."

She laughed. "You keep it safe, and one day maybe you can hand it on."

"What do I do with it?"

"You wear it. The old man said it attracts what you need." She snapped her fingers. "Gilles. That was his name. Great-Grand-Pere Gilles. His wife was Juliana. I was named after her." She stretched up on tiptoe the way Lucy did and fastened the feather to his shirt with the tiny gold pin.

"Won't people think I'm odd to wear a white feather?"

"Most people won't notice it." She shrugged and then she whispered, "Your grandad never did, but he came to me anyway. It's a fairy thing."

Dequan kissed her and Grandad Li, shook hands with Uncle Adam Tan, and nodded to Aunt Cherie. Giving her a nephewly kiss might be bad for his health.

He retreated to his flat, where he went to bed early. No use texting Lucy.

Fucking like bunnies, Lucy had said, with such relish! It must be an in-joke she shared with her lover.

Dequan was the one who mostly shared her in-jokes, so she'd said it to him out of old habit. She wouldn't think twice. They'd always been able to tell one another anything.

He couldn't imagine a girlfriend *fucking like bunnies* with him.

Maybe Tamzin Herrick would have if they'd ever got as far as a bed. Tamzin was lovely, daft and elf-obsessed, and she and Dequan had been inseparable during their last year of school. Her family had moved just after Tamzin graduated.

In occasional paranoid moments, he wondered if that had anything to do with him. Did the respectable Herricks not want grandchildren who would be a mix of Dutch, Chinese and possibly something else on their father's side?

And now Lucy was leaving, too.

It was ridiculous to mind. He never saw much of her, but she was always *there,* as a promise of companionship. They got one another.

He didn't envy Lucy's man. He didn't love Lucy *that* way.

After Tamzin, he'd never felt more than affection for any girlfriend, not even for the tall and elegant Puck Verhoven who should have been perfect in every way.

For the first time, he entertained the thought that maybe his girlfriends had a point. Maybe the Dequan and Lucy dynamic *was* to blame for his lack of commitment. Lucy got him in a way his girlfriends didn't. He supposed the converse was also true. And now she had Paris, who lit her up like Christmas.

He sat up, located his phone, and tapped the *contacts* icon.

"Calling Puck," the phone remarked.

After a few rings, the call connected. "Hello?"

"Hello, Puck. It's Dequan."

"This, I know," she said patiently.

"Merry Christmas."

"Thank you." Her voice was cool, and he visualised her crossing her long legs and tucking a lock of hair behind her ear. Or maybe she was in bed. *Oops.*

"Is this a bad time?"

"No. Was there something you wanted to say, Dequan?"

"I hope you had a good Christmas."

"I did. Joop and his family are visiting."

"Great. I'm glad. He's a nice guy."

"I think so." There was another brief pause, and then she said, "I hope you had a happy day."

"Not especially," he admitted.

"I'm sorry. But maybe —" She broke off.

"Maybe?"

"No, it is not my business now."

"Tell me anyway?"

He saw her in his mind's eye, biting her lower lip in thought and then she said, "You know how you are always putting someone in the way of something they want."

"Yes." The finder's fees he charged kept him comfortably solvent.

"Maybe you should think about what *you* want, and put yourself in the way of it."

"Oh?"

"It seems to me that you know what others want, but for you, when you have something good, you look for some reason not to want it."

"I do see that," he said quietly. "Puck, I'm sorry I hurt you."

"Don't be sorry. My ego is a little bruised, but my heart is not. One day you'll find someone. You'll be with her because your heart will know what your head doesn't. If you find her, be *hers*."

"Thank you. I'll try," he said.

"Merry Christmas, *mijn vriend*," Puck said.

"Let's catch up for coffee one day soon. Joop, too."

"I don't think so . . . but I do wish you well," she said and cut the call.

Dequan lay down again. Puck had probably not been pleased to hear from him so soon after their breakup, but she had given him good advice. She'd also cut him loose. He wondered if that was to do with Joop. He *was* a nice guy.

Burned my bridges with that one.

Dequan thought of Lucy.

My Lucy-Lou.

He gently closed the door on her. She was still his favourite person in the world, but he was no longer hers. Not only had she fallen in love with the man called Paris, but she'd deliberately made a baby with him. Lucy would never do that if she weren't in that relationship for the long haul. Ergo, the days of spag tom were probably over.

He sighed. If he'd known about Paris and Lucy, he mightn't have broken it off with Puck. She was intelligent, beautiful, elegant, thoughtful and innately kind, even if she didn't do the *fuck like bunnies* thing.

And that would have been self-serving and unfair.

So, Dequan, what the hell do you want?

He went to sleep, still wondering.

Chapter Five: Linda

One day before Martina Bless saw the gooseman at Patterdale market, mislaid her café staff and found a message on a napkin, Dequan's phone chimed as a text came in.

He was in a feather bed. A beguiling woman with long brown hair and a laughing mouth was doing delicious things to his balls. The bed was in a chalet-style room. There was a pretty Christmas quilt that looked hand-made. He planned to examine that in detail when his glorious interlude came to a natural lull. He smelled the piquant tang of coffee and chocolate. For some reason, he thought the woman was German.

She was sucking him, loving it as much as he was.

Wait – I'm – ooohhh . . .

He squirmed and went right out of his head.

Yes-yes –

Ping!

Another text landed.

He moaned in protest as the delightful woman lifted her head. "Better deal with that, Liebling."

She was right. Those texts were important.

Might be Lucy.

Ow – go down, cock!

Dequan groped for the phone and squinted at the screen. He read the later of the two texts.

V-S Pick-up in ten.

What?

The earlier one was no more informative.

V-S Pick-up in fifteen.

He was uncomfortably hard, and his companion had vanished with the dream.

I needed two more minutes. Maybe one. Now I'll have to fix myself.

The texts clicked into context in his mind as he remembered the Vouch-Safe voucher Lucy had modified for him. He'd agreed to leave on Boxing Day and — he eyed the numbers on the phone — it had been Boxing Day for a whole four hours and fifty-three minutes.

Five o-freaking-clock pick-up! Seriously?

No time to wank, then.

He got out of bed and hauled on yesterday's clothes, still clean after that peculiar Christmas dinner.

There was no time to pack, but that was the point of Vouch-Safe vouchers. Since the clients didn't know where they were going, they took the bare necessities. Anything they needed but couldn't be expected to know they needed was provided by the company.

He blundered into the bathroom, used the loo, splashed his face, trod into his shoes and grabbed his toiletries, then added jacket, spare shirt, jocks and shorts grabbed at random from the clothes horse.

Déjà vu. He'd done this when he attempted to use the original voucher, though that hadn't been five in the morning.

He bundled everything into a holdall and pocketed his wallet and phone. He had no time for coffee or a shower, so he took the last bunch of grapes for breakfast-on-the-run and left the flat. He dropped the key in the holdall as he turned to face the silent street.

A long car glided around the corner and came to rest beside him.

He blinked at the headlights as the driver got out. She was several years older than him. She had on jeans and a lighter blouse, and dark hair tied back in a tail. She wasn't the driver who'd rejected the voucher before.

As she stepped under a streetlight, he saw a logo on her top pocket. *V-S.*

She was holding a tablet, which she tapped. "Qin, mystery holiday voucher, party of one?"

"Yes. I'm Dequan Qin," he said, juggling the holdall and pushing his phone into his pocket. His balls ached, which was disconcerting. "Do you need to see my booking confirmation?"

"A shareholder used her code, so you're pre-confirmed." She glanced at the tablet again. "Are you ready to go, Mister Qin?"

Her tone implied that he'd better be.

Dequan stepped towards the car.

The woman said, "Luggage?"

He relinquished his holdall. She put it in the boot and then opened the rear passenger door.

So, he was to be chauffeured in solitary style. Dequan got in and did up his seatbelt.

"Ready?" the driver asked in her cool, neutral voice.

"I am. May I ask why you came so early?"

You might have given me a chance to finish that close encounter of the fräulein *kind.*

For a few seconds, he thought she wouldn't answer, but then she said, "We have a long drive, and I would prefer to get home in daylight." She put the car into gear and pulled out into the quiet street.

"You live here in Sydney?"

She paused again.

"I'm not planning to stalk you," Dequan said.

"Good. My husband bites." She drew a sudden and audible breath. "Forget I said that. My name's Linda."

"Good morning, Linda."

"I was at the Sydney office when your voucher was activated on the twenty-fourth. The dispatcher said I might as well service it. And that's the last piece of information I can give you."

The car's exterior looked like any other large sedan. The inside was more of a surprise. He poked about, opening cupboards and a padded lid in the console. He found food and drink, reading matter, a pillow, a rug, a small sound system and a temperature control. He ate his grapes and then some of the supplies, including a fresh flask of coffee. After an hour or so, he realised the sun must have risen, but the light in the car hadn't changed.

"Linda?"

"Yes?" She didn't move her head, but he supposed she might have glanced in the rearview mirror.

"I can't see out the windows."

"You're not supposed to. It's no mystery if you see where you're going."

He took out his phone. *Out of service.*

Dequan looked at it thoughtfully.

"Linda?"

"Yes?"

"My phone's not working."

"It's all right, Mister Qin. It will be fine when we reach our destination. Probably. Mostly. Why not sleep?"

Asking questions was unprofitable, so he closed his eyes.

Maybe I'll find the fräulein *again and finish what we started.*

His balls throbbed. *Yes, please.*

Better not. I might moan and thrash about, and Linda would disapprove.

Travel to a holiday destination was usually passed in pleasant anticipation, or in discomfort and delays. Dequan found anticipation difficult. He had no clue where he was going. Linda had said it was a long drive, and that she wanted to be home in daylight. If Linda lived near his destination, then they might be travelling all day. If she had a long drive home after decanting him, then they might arrive by lunchtime.

"Linda?"

"I can't tell you anything more, Mister Qin. We'll have a comfort stop soon."

He retorted, "You mean this car *doesn't* have an on-board loo?"

"The V-S vans do. Using a van for a single voucher makes no sense, economically speaking." She paused for a beat and then added, "There's a wide-necked bottle if you're desperate. I won't peep."

"So—"

"Mister Qin, if you persist in trying to engage me in conversation, I'll raise the privacy screens."

Dequan whistled between his teeth, feeling admonished. He didn't mind. He enjoyed verbal sparring and tart-tongued women. After a while, despite his reservations, he went to sleep.

Chapter Six: Questions

Dequan woke to discover the car had stopped. Linda opened the door and enquired civilly if he needed that comfort break.

No moans then. He couldn't remember his dreams, if any.

Blinking, he got out of the car and looked about. Beyond the petrol station where they were parked, the highway stretched on between scrubby trees and open land. "Where are we?"

"At the service station."

"I can see that."

Linda said, "Go and do whatever. Don't buy coffee. I restocked supplies and petrol while you topped up your beauty sleep. Hurry."

She's going to allow me unsupervised into a public place! He glanced at the petrol pumps. She'd filled up while he slumbered. Really? The automatic door opened, and he stepped in. A grey-haired woman sat behind the counter, playing chess against herself. "Good morning, Mister Qin."

"Good morning." Her use of his name registered. Linda had obviously briefed her.

"The restroom is through there."

When he came out, the woman had checkmated herself. She looked up at him. "Goose," she remarked.

"I wouldn't be that hard on yourself. Maybe you lost, but

31

you won as well."

"Have a nice day, Mister Qin."

"You, too . . . um . . ."

"Elvie." She tapped a badge on her shirt.

"Elvie." Dequan returned to the car.

Linda was leaning on the door, drinking coffee.

He stared at her. She stared back. Even over the pervasive scent of coffee, he perceived she smelled of tea roses. She looked to be in her forties, and she was tall and athletic. He had the odd feeling he wasn't really seeing her. Or maybe he wasn't seeing the real her. Childhood memories, prompted by his conversations with Lucy and Gran Qin, bubbled up in his mind.

"Linda, are you using a glamour?"

Her eyebrows went up. "I've never been asked that before."

"I mean, are you using some power to make me perceive what isn't true?"

She seemed to consider her words before responding. "I'm not. However, I *am* dialled down."

"Ah."

"You understand the term?"

"You've damped down your presence. You're flying under the radar."

"I always do it when I'm at work."

Dequan said, "My cousin works as a camp companion on Ferris Island. Once we went into a shop. And one of the assistants served her without a second glance. Lucy said later they'd spent two months together at camp."

"There you are, then."

"Is your name really Linda? Lucy uses pseudonyms at work."

"Really, Linda. I haven't told you any lies."

"Will you show me your real self?"

"No."

"Will you come to bed with me?"

Oops. That popped out.

"Not a chance. I have an exciting and excitable husband."

"Are you a fairy?"

"I'm a halfling. Who gave you that terrifying goose feather?"

"If I tell you will you—"

"Pretend I didn't ask. Get in the car and behave yourself."

"Just one thing. It has nothing to do with the voucher, or with you."

She held up a finger. "One question. Then I don't want another peep out of you."

He assembled the question carefully. "My cousin is having a baby."

"My felicitations. Yours?"

"No. The father is half human and half waterfolk, and he can't breathe properly in Sydney. Will the baby be able to?"

Linda appeared to think about that for a while. Finally, she said. "I don't know. My husband's half-brother is a water halfling. He's even more excitable than my husband. He finds it challenging to spend much time in the human realm. His children are a mixed bunch. Two of them are at home anywhere. One—not so much. The baby is too young to tell, but I suspect she'll turn heads and unsettle nerves wherever she goes. Their mother isn't particularly human either, so in your cousin's case, I couldn't hazard a guess. Now, *in*."

Dequan got in the car.

He wished he'd met Linda in other circumstances. She was a maze of contradictions, and he'd always enjoyed mazes. It was a pity about the husband. Otherwise, he might have hoped *she* was the holiday mystery. Still . . .

"Linda?"

"Yes?"

"When this is over, will you come out with me for a drink?

Bring your husband, too."

He waited for her to snap, but she just said, "Thank you for the invitation, Mister Qin. I'd enjoy seeing you and my husband in the same room. You're almost as annoying as he is."

"Yes, then?"

"No. It's against regulations and the non-fraternisation rule is developing a nasty bend already. I like you. You remind me of our son, although he's younger. That means I want to answer your questions and kiss the top of your head. That's not supposed to happen and it's not appropriate. Therefore—"

There was a subtle shift in the atmosphere in the vehicle.

"Linda?"

There was no reply, and after a moment he realised Linda must have engaged the privacy screen.

CHAPTER SEVEN: GEESE AT JOURNEY'S END

Dequan, Patterdale, December Twenty-sixth, Saint Stephen's Day

The car stopped again in the afternoon. Linda directed Dequan to another service station, where another attendant knew his name.

They drove for another three or so hours before Linda brought the car to a halt.

When she opened the door, she had Dequan's bag in her hand.

"Journey's end, Mister Qin." She slid a hand into her pocket and pulled out a booklet.

Raffle tickets?

Linda caught his eye. "This book of chits is part of the deal. Use whatever you please." She pointed behind him. "You're booked in at the *Over Here B&B*, just across the road, for five nights. At the end of the time, a driver will text you an eta. You'll need to be ready. He, or she, will return you to your pick-up point. Any questions?"

Dequan accepted the book of tickets and his bag. "What happens if I want to go home early, or later? Can I call you?"

"Nice try, Mister Qin. The contract is locked in. Enjoy your stay." She got back into the car.

Dequan watched her drive away. He had no idea where he was, but the trip had lasted over twelve hours, including breaks. The weather was cooler than it had been in Sydney.

The air was pleasantly fresh, and he decided he was either in a leafy suburb or possibly a country town. Judging by the travel time, the temperature, the architecture, and the vegetation, he thought he was probably in Victoria.

He pulled out his phone and then put it away. It was online again, but there was no one he wanted to call, except for Lucy, who was out of range *fucking like bunnies* with her beloved, who lived in a place where electronics didn't work.

His home for the next few days was a quaint old house tucked in a well-established garden. As mystery holiday destinations went, it seemed pedestrian, but it should be restful.

Dequan decided he'd spend the break walking, exploring and pondering Puck's advice.

"Think about what you want. Put yourself in the way of it."
Excellent idea.
So — what do you want, Dequan?

He opened the garden gate with a click and walked along the path to the house, under the hanging sign saying *Over Here B&B*. The gardens were charming and so peaceful he felt as if he'd wandered into a favourite storybook.

Gran would love this place. So would Mum and Lucy.

He mounted five mossy steps, and he was about to ring the bell for admittance when someone honked behind him.

Linda?

Dequan turned, almost falling off the top step as a wave of large white birds tore up after him and milled around his feet.

He dropped the holdall and clutched at the door.

More honks rang out as the birds who'd been underneath the holdall scattered, shooting him filthy looks as they went. They right-about-turned and marched back to his feet.

He regained his balance, unable to take a step for fear of treading on a bird.

That would serve them right, but he had no desire to lose a kneecap. They looked capable of anything.

He looked down at the milling flock. His heart pounded,

but when they didn't attack, he realised his first impression of a dozen or more was wrong. There were six. They were white. Their large feet were a menacing shade of orange and so were their bills. Their eyes were orange, too.

He lifted a cautious foot.

Immediately, six bills opened and hissed in unison. The birds snaked their heads, and he had the impression they were trying to drive him down the steps.

"I'm allowed to be here. I have a booking," he told them. He lowered his foot and bent to pick up the holdall.

The hissing intensified.

Okay. We won't be doing that, then.

He tugged the bellpull, producing melodious chimes.

The door swung open.

Dequan stumbled through into the foyer and washed up in a room with a sign saying *reception*.

A man looked up from his seat behind the counter. Dequan had just time to see he wore a calico cat around his neck like a shawl before the white birds charged in after him and all hell broke loose.

Dequan staggered as he got a buffet from a wing that meant business.

"Great bogle!" The man sprang to his feet and yelled as the cat, dislodged by the movement, dug in its claws. "Ow! *Must* you do that, Calico?"

The cat vanished, and a woman with strawberry blonde hair in a neat roll stood up from below the counter. She was naked.

"Whoa!" Dequan felt his mouth open in a violent cocktail of emotions.

The man, who had been clutching his shoulder, glanced at Dequan and whipped a blanket off the chair where he'd been sitting.

Dequan noticed distractedly that it was patterned with holly leaves.

The man draped the blanket around the woman before staring at Dequan and the birds. "What the fuck?"

The woman burst into a peal of laughter. "'tis your dad's fault, darlin'."

"Undoubtedly." The man held up one finger to Dequan and raised his voice over the cacophony of honking and hissing.

"You are our V-S guest, Dequan Qin. Is that right?"

Dequan nodded, wide-eyed.

The man, who was dark-haired with a touch of grey at his temples, said, "We need to deal with this situation." He tilted his head and called, "Dad!"

The door was still open, but the bell jangled again as an elderly man stormed up the steps. He had iron-grey hair and his eyes flashed an intense turquoise. He stopped just inside the door.

"Wondered where those fuckers charged off to." He turned his attention to Dequan. "What the fuck did you do to my geese, man?"

Geese? Of course. That's what they were.

"Nothing."

The man's jaw came out in an argumentative way. "You must have fucking well done something to attract them!"

The other man sighed. "Dad, I don't care who did what. Just take them away. Calypso, will you book Mister Qin in while Dad and I remove these birds from the premises?"

The older man looked about to argue but the other one, presumably his son, snapped his fingers.

The geese stopped yammering.

"All right, friends. Leave Mister Qin alone. Show's over." He pointed to the door.

The geese shuffled their feet and seemed to confer.

"Out!" the dark man said.

The two men stepped outside and vanished down the

steps, with the flock parading after. One snaked its head around to fix Dequan with an orange eye.

Later.

"What was that about?" Dequan asked.

The woman laughed. "Fay geese. Some whim of my father-by-love. Usually, it's fay goats in the copse. Let's book you in." She produced an old-fashioned visitors' book from under the counter and pushed it towards Dequan, along with a pen.

Bemused, he signed his name and dated it.

"Welcome to *Over Here B&B*," the woman said.

He saw she had odd-coloured eyes. One was amber and the other sea green. She seemed unfazed that he'd seen her naked and that she was now wearing a blanket.

"I'm Calypso. My own name is Lindon, but I'm also Mistress Peckerdale, because I'm married to Kris," she said. "Do you have a bag?"

Dequan went out and retrieved his bag. He expected it to be filthy, but it was unmolested. There was no sign the geese had ever been there. He wondered if he'd hallucinated them.

"We put you in the alp room on the second floor." Calypso handed him a key. It was an actual key, not a key card.

Dequan headed up the stairs. He glanced back once, but Calypso had gone. The calico cat was back, purring on the blanket which was again draped over the chair.

Chapter Eight: The Alp Room

Dequan, Patterdale, December Twenty-sixth, Saint Stephen's Day

The stairs were lined with paintings. Dequan decided to look at them later. He climbed a second flight and located the right room.

Alp room. He wondered if there was a real alp somewhere. After those geese and the odd people he'd encountered, he wouldn't be surprised.

Alp. He remembered the *fräulein*. *Oh.* Dreams had to come from somewhere, and he wondered where that glorious armful originated. She was nothing like Lucy. Just as well. That would be inappropriate. She was nothing like any of his girlfriends.

Well, maybe a little like Puck, who was tall, elegant and fair, but Puck had never sucked his balls and she lived in a minimalist flat with a healthy slatted bed.

Better not think of that *fräulein*. He refused to spend his first few minutes in the B&B bedroom wrestling with a hard-on.

He must have invented the *fräulein*. He hadn't got any since breaking with Puck, so maybe he'd been comforting his balls in his sleep, and his subconscious had kindly provided a partner in pleasure.

He shook the idea away and opened the door. He stepped into an airy room appointed to look like a Swiss chalet.

There was indeed an alp! It was a *trompe l'oeil* that occupied the whole rear wall. It was breathtaking. Dequan wanted to step right into the picture and scramble up that shining mountainside to the chalet at the top, where he might find a feather bed and the *fräulein*. Undoubtedly, she would be there, awaiting his pleasure and hers.

He fancied he could smell mocha and feel her warm breath on his thighs.

Ugh. Get down, cock. Stop thinking of her.

He stared at the scene for a while, going close to the painting and squinting up at the chalet. By the trick of perspective, it seemed far away as well as high above his head. Binoculars might bring it into focus. Pity he hadn't thought to bring any.

Someone stood at the window, leaning out over a window box of flowers. He held his breath and willed his focus to sharpen. He couldn't make out the face or even the sex, but he knew perfectly well who it was.

Come on, Fräulein. *Reach out your hands and I'll jump into the painting.*

When his eyes began to ache, he stepped back and then turned his attention to the window that looked out onto the real view. He looked down at a sleepy summer garden. Since he was upstairs, he gazed over and through the smaller trees and into the street beyond. There were a couple of shops and a two-storey square building styling itself *Thymelines Gallery*.

Aha! Maybe someone from there had wrought the stair paintings and the mighty and illusory alp.

He put his bag on the bed and sat beside it. His eyebrows shot up as he took in the perfectly sprung mattress. This one wasn't feathers. He wasn't sure what it was.

A pottery crock on the bedside table revealed tiny spiced biscuits that smelled like the *speculaas* his mother made as a nod to her heritage. A closer look revealed the biscuits were shaped like dancers, swans, and hens. There was also at least one goose.

I can eat the twelve days of Christmas!

He ate the goose before wondering about dinner. It must be half-past five or six o'clock by now and he wanted something more substantial than biscuits.

There was no internal phone in the room, and he didn't see a menu. There was a small bathroom, so he showered quickly. He opened his holdall to put on his fresh shirt and discovered to his consternation that he'd put in the old favourite which Lucy had ripped from hem to collar to prevent him from wearing it again. He'd tossed it in the wash with the idea of giving it to his mother as an ingredient for her next memory quilt.

He restored it to the holdall and put on his other shirt again. He'd go shopping tomorrow. This was an all-provided holiday, but he couldn't expect the couple from reception to give him a shirt. The woman, Calypso, had an odd idea of clothing, for a start.

He inspected himself in the bathroom mirror.

He was clean, but the white feather Gran Qin had given him had better come off. This shirt was going to be washed as soon as he sourced a new one and he didn't want to ruin the peculiar heirloom.

He tried to undo the gold pin. The catch that Gran Qin's tiny hands had managed so adeptly resisted his efforts at grip and manipulation.

Dequan gave up. He slipped out of the shirt and put on his light jacket over bare skin. It would do for tonight.

He stuck his wallet and phone in his pocket along with the door key and ventured downstairs to reception.

"We don't serve dinner, darlin'," Calypso said when he enquired.

"Oh." Of course not. This was a bed-and-breakfast, not a motel.

She looked at him with sympathy. This time, she had on an amber-coloured dress. He had the unnerving feeling it might slip off her shoulder at any time. She must be at least as old as her husband, but she was one of the most alluring women he'd ever met.

Timeless. That was the adjective for people like her. No doubt she'd been beautiful all her life and beauty had become a habit. She had an accent he thought was Irish and she smelled of some sleepy garden plant.

"Plenty of places serve food," she said. "There's free soup and bread at Peckerdale Grene Tower . . . though that's a bit of a walk from here. I recommend the *Pride of Erin* bar. They do a good counter tea if you like traditional cooking. *Fee Kaffee* is close by, but they don't do dinner."

"I—"

Her voice flowed on. "Kris made maps."

She ducked under the counter, moving with a speed and grace that reminded him of Lucy in her pre-pregnancy days.

"Here!" She popped up triumphantly and leaned over the counter in a waft of that sleepy perfume to hand him a paper.

He spread it out. He supposed it was a map, but it was more like an artist's impression of a precinct, with thumbnail drawings of buildings labelled in minuscule print. It was a beautiful thing.

"You'll need a magnifying glass for that," someone said.

Dequan turned to face a man in his thirties, brown haired, tall, and sporting odd eyes like Calypso's. Unlike her fair, faintly freckled skin, his was an odd shade of olive.

The man smiled and offered his hand. "Corin Peckerdale. I work here now and then, but mostly I'm at the gallery."

Dequan accepted his hand and shook. This one smelled of ripe figs. He was beginning to catch on to a trend.

Corin nodded towards the counter. "Calypso's my mother, and Kris, who made the maps, is my father. He tends to mess up the size of the print. Mama—" He turned back to the woman. "There are magnifiers in the gallery. Here." He flicked his fingers and handed a small folding glass to Dequan. "I'm off now. If you need anything this week, leave a note at reception. I'll be around. Otherwise, you can pop over to the gallery." He jerked his head towards the door. "Right, Mama, I'll see you later."

Calypso hitched herself over the counter like a gymnast and hugged her son. "Have you seen your dad, darlin'? He and Peter P were dealing with geese."

"Geese?" Corin visibly checked himself and put a finger to his mother's lips. "No, don't tell me." He disengaged and raised an eyebrow at Dequan. "This place tends to be odd at times. I hope you won't hold it against us." He went out with a jangle of bells from the door.

Dequan, armed with the map and the powerful magnifying glass, turned to take his leave of Calypso, but she must have ducked back under the counter. The calico cat was perched on the visitors' book, licking one neat paw. She blinked placidly at Dequan and he perceived she, too, had mismatched eyes.

Good God! These people colour-coordinated their cat?

Dequan walked down the steps and through the garden. It was so quiet he might have been in the depths of the country. He stepped out through the gate into the buzz of light traffic. He examined the map and oriented himself, remembering too late he needn't have bothered. He could use his phone to navigate.

He thumbed the phone on and remembered he still didn't know where he was.

He typed in a search for *Thymelines Gallery* and *Over Here B&B*.

The answer popped up in seconds.

Patterdale. He skimmed the information and learned it was a town in south-east Victoria, not far from the larger centre of Appledore. It held the *Counterpoint* music festival in April and was home to the *Forever* dancing troupe and the indie bands *Sunshower* and *4TsQuad*. So now he knew.

Take that, no-questions-Linda! He compared the map on his

phone with the artistic rendition he'd acquired from the B&B. After a few seconds, he tucked his phone back in his pocket. He might as well save the battery.

Dammit! He'd forgotten to pack his charger.

He navigated himself to the pub, a new building called the *Pride of Erin*. He had a tiny glass of poteen, which was interesting, and he ate dinner in exchange for one of the chits. The barmaid gave him a mischievous smile and a babble of incomprehensible suggestions for his entertainment over the next week. She was tiny, and she spoke with the same accent as Calypso. Corin's sister? He resolved to watch his tongue. Small town people probably all knew one another. Offend one and you'd offend them all.

After dinner, he wandered the streets, wishing Lucy was with him. She would have enjoyed the whole enterprise, but she'd got a better offer.

It had been a long day, so he returned to the B&B.

The calico cat was on the counter, and she paused in her industrious washing to watch as he headed for the stairs. "Goodnight," he said. It seemed the natural thing to do.

CHAPTER NINE: RETURN OF THE GEESE

Dequan, Patterdale, December Twenty-seventh

On his first and last morning at the *Over Here B&B*, Dequan woke early after a confusing dream of geese, poteen, cats and feathers with a disturbing side-dish of *fräulein* in a feather bed. This time, to his disappointment, they hadn't got beyond some innovative foreplay involving feathers. His cock was flexing in anticipation, but at least he didn't have a raging hard-on to deal with this morning.

Typical! I have the time today and nowhere I have to be.

He lay in the soft light coming from the window and contemplated the alp on the wall. Presumably, the figure at the chalet was responsible for the *fräulein*'s starring role in his dreams.

He dressed and then dragged a carved wooden chair across the room. It was sturdy enough to stand on and should bring his eyes up level with the chalet so he could ply the magnifying glass Corin had given him.

He had a hand on the wall preparatory to mounting the chair when a tap on the door made him freeze. "Yes?"

"Room service."

There was no time to drag the chair back, but he retreated to sit on the bed as if about to put his shoes on. "Come in."

Corin Peckerdale edged in, carrying a tray of tea things. "If this is too early, I can bring it later tomorrow," he said.

"It's okay." Dequan ran his fingers through his hair, not looking at the chair although there was no reason to be embarrassed. He couldn't be the first person who'd wanted a close look at that beautiful painting. "What's happening in Patterdale at this hour?"

Corin shrugged. "Not a lot. There's a summer market a few streets over if you feel like doing that."

"I might as well," Dequan said, though he doubted a small-town market could hold a candle to the ones he knew in Sydney.

Corin set the tray on the bedside table. "What brings you to Patterdale?" he asked.

Dequan considered telling him the story of the exchanged voucher, Lucy, Puck, Linda and everything else. He decided against it. "Post-Christmas break. Why?"

"We registered for Vouch-Safe travellers in November. You're our first taker. I'm trying to get a feeling for V-S travellers and why they might choose us," Corin said.

"I left it up to V-S to pick the destination. I assume your name came out of the hat because you had an opening that fitted my last-minute request for Boxing Day travel. V-S guarantee to give you the dates you want, but that means you depend on someone having vacancies—" Aware he might sound ungracious, he added, "My cousin works for a V-S subsidiary, and their camps are always fully booked well ahead. She pulled strings and teed this up for me."

Corin said, "I hope you enjoy your time with us. Things sometimes get a bit—"

"Odd. So you said." Dequan added, "You're a fairy, aren't you?"

"What gave me away? My complexion?" Corin ran a hand over his olive cheek.

"My V-S driver was one. She, you and your mother all have what my grandmother calls *le bouquet de fees*. Also, I saw you conjure that magnifying glass for me yesterday."

"Oops."

"You were discreet, but I have a friend who conjures, so I believe my eyes rather than thinking it's a trick of the light. And your mother is rather—" He stopped, aware he was about to say something inappropriate.

"My mama is indeed *rather,* in both her forms. Leppy colleens come on rather strong. Don't let it trouble you."

"Both her forms?"

"Oops," Corin said again.

"I won't let it trouble me." He added, cautiously, "Are all the staff here fairies?"

"Mostly. Don't worry about it. I promise we won't put a compulsion on you or turn you into a toad."

"I know." He decided to show off a little. "The first would be bad manners and the second is impossible."

Corin raised a hand. "*Touche!* You mentioned a friend who conjures. I assume that's how you know about us?"

"Otto explained some details, but I've always known. One of my ancestors was a courtfolk man, so you might say I *am* one of you in a very minor way."

"Most of us don't advertise what we are if we live this side of the gates," Corin said. He turned to go. "I'll tell the others not to worry about *passing,* since you're okay with it. Is there anything you need by voucher or in friendship?"

"A charging cable for my phone would be useful. I left mine behind."

"I can get that for you. You may have noticed your phone doesn't work well in the B&B. It's on account of the wards. It will be fine outside our gates." He went out, closing the door with an ostentatious flick of his fingers.

Well, well. Life just got that bit more interesting. Gran will be delighted when I tell her about this place.

Dequan glanced back at the alp, but his desire to climb on the chair had dissipated. Corin might pop back in and start talking again. He was drinking his tea when a charging cord blinked into being on the tray. Obviously, Corin was taking him at his word.

Only the calico cat was in reception when he went down-stairs. "Good morning. I'm going to the market."

The calico cat licked a paw and ran it over an ear.

Oh well, he didn't expect a cat to speak to him, even a col-our-coordinated cat in an establishment run by fairies.

He opened the door and sauntered down the five mossy steps.

The fresh summer morning greeted him, and he felt a surge of freedom. He was in a new environment. He'd left his phone charging, so no one could contact him this morning. It was unexpectedly liberating to be alone. He could do whatever he wanted for the next few days.

He walked down the path through the garden and then, on a whim, turned back to see if he could spot the alp room win-dow.

Just in case the fräulein *has magically appeared.*

Honk! The goose brigade stormed into view and sur-rounded him with darting necks, hissing bills, and tramping orange feet.

Dammit! "Back off!"

The geese continued to mill around.

He tried to remember how Kris had dealt with them, be-yond hollering *Dad* to summon the irascible old man. Had he clicked his fingers?

Dequan clicked his fingers.

The cacophony continued.

"Go away! Back off!" He waved his arms and turned to eye the steps. He could leap and make a dash for it, trusting to luck that he wouldn't land on a goose. He prepared to launch, but the nearest goose aimed a vicious peck at his shin. It missed, but Dequan rethought his options.

Yelling for help was ignominious. Besides, he was an adult. He refused to be outmanoeuvred by six geese, even if they were bigger, meaner, and more intellectual than the average bird of their type. He had no doubt they were intellectual. Those orange eyes fairly sparkled with notions.

If he couldn't get to the steps, what about the gate? That was just three or so paces behind him. Wild geese could fly, but he thought domestic ones didn't.

He shuffled in a semi-circular turn.

"Right, you." He took a pace towards the gate, and then another. A third step brought him to the gate, and he clicked it open, shimmied through and closed it as quickly as he could.

Serve you right if you bang your bills.

He turned right at random and set off.

The beating of wide wings informed him these geese could indeed fly. They flapped overhead, combing his hair with their claws, and flustered to land in front of him.

Dequan stopped.

The geese eyed him with orange intensity.

He stepped forward.

Bills stabbed in his direction.

Okay, back through the gate.

He spun on his heels and headed back the short distance to the B&B gate. It was a daft situation. If this was what Corin Peckerdale chose to term *a little bit odd,* he could keep it. If the fairy collective at *Over Here B&B* expected a good review on the Vouch-Safe site, they could whistle for it.

He put a hand on the gate and let go with a curse when a goose levitated to the latch and hissed at him.

His options had shrunk to screaming for help or finding somewhere goose-proof to go to ground. He chose the latter, stepping out as fast as he could.

The geese were right behind him, but to his surprise, they stopped hissing and honking. Maybe they needed all their breath to keep up with his strides. He came to a park and spotted a low concrete-built public convenience.

Goose-proof, surely. He could go to ground in there and phone the B&B for someone, probably Kris, to come and rescue him.

I'm trapped in the loo being menaced by geese. Good one, Dequan. Very manly.

Oops! He'd left his phone in the alp room. Surely someone with a phone would soon come to unlock the loo.

He was almost level with the building, and he slid his gaze sideways to gauge the optimum time to—

He swerved sideways and made a dash. The geese set up their hissing, honking, and flapping, but he had his hand on the door.

It was locked. The sign said, *Open seven am to nine pm.*

Dequan turned to face the geese. They made no move to attack.

Slowly he put up his hands. "I give up. What do you guys *want*?"

One of the geese flipped its tail. A look of steely concentration came over its eyes and, to his horrified amusement, it laid an egg.

"So, what do you *gals* want?"

The goose responsible for the egg stared at it and then, comically, nudged the thing to roll over his shoe.

"You want me to carry your egg. I suppose you want me to hatch it, too?" Slowly, he bent and reached for the egg. It was a lot bigger than a duck egg, which was only reasonable, and it was warm. Distractedly, he put it in his top pocket and hoped it wouldn't break. It was a very tight fit.

One of the geese snapped at his ankle.

Cowering against the door of the public convenience was not a good look. He thought it was still quite a while before seven o'clock, so he returned to the footpath.

His escort fell in behind, shooing him along.

They're driving me.

The conclusion was unbelievable, but at least it explained

why they hadn't truly attacked him.

Two blocks down from his abortive effort to shelter in the loo, they reached the market.

Mentally, he apologised for his patronising assessment. It was a great deal bigger than he'd expected, with stalls and vans set up over a large area. There was a lot of what he thought of as after-Christmas produce. If he could dodge the geese, he could get breakfast.

He plunged into the aisle between the first set of stalls, hoping the geese would be scared off by the merchants setting up. They did pause to poke about in some spilled vegetable refuse, but when he edged away, their attention snapped back to him.

He slowed down again and spoke to a man unloading lettuces so fresh he could smell their slightly bitter scent. "Excuse me . . . do you know anything about geese?"

"Not much, cobber. The livestock area's that-a-way." He jerked a thumb.

"Shouldn't think you'll find geese there, though there were some before Christmas. Turkeys, too," someone else said helpfully.

A bill butted Dequan's ankle. He moved on hurriedly.

He was taking a forced tour of the market, but nobody else seemed to notice anything amiss. He supposed they thought he was taking his pets for a walk.

He looked about for someone sensible with a phone so he could call the B&B. Presumably, the desk phone worked. Otherwise, how could they take bookings?

Chapter Ten: Enter the Fräulein

Dequan, Patterdale, December Twenty-seventh

A s the geese hustled him along, Dequan spotted a familiar figure.

It was the pretty barmaid from the *Pride of Erin* where he'd got dinner last night. He half raised a hand and then froze when he saw her turn aside to accost a tall woman with light brown hair. She had an old-fashioned basket over each arm, and he had the impression she had just turned, so he'd missed seeing her face by a half-second.

She had a beautiful figure, buxom without being fulsome, and her hair was a soft shade that was obviously natural. She exchanged a few words with the barmaid, and he admired her grace and strength. The baskets were full of produce, but she held them as if they were light.

He realised his mouth had gone dry and he was gawking like a schoolboy.

It's the fräulein. *It bloody is. It's the* fräulein. My *feather bed* fräulein.

The thought was decided and unpremeditated.

"Don't be silly," he told himself, but his gaze seemed glued to the enticing woman.

Before he could pull himself together and get her attention, she nodded to the barmaid and turned, hips swaying, to disappear into the crowd.

Dequan looked down at the geese. They stared back. One of them looked a bit unfocused. As he watched, it lowered its rear end and laid an egg.

"I don't have room in my pocket for that one," he said.

The geese stared. Slowly, he bent and picked it up.

A third goose lost focus.

Another egg. This was well past ridiculous. And the *fräulein* had vanished in the crowd. He wanted to stamp his foot. If he trod on a goose, that was the goose's bad luck.

"You should put those in a poke," a voice said from beside him.

He looked down at the barmaid from the *Pride of Erin*. She dimpled up at him. She was no taller than Lucy, but unlike his pocket-sized cousin, this one had red hair and a fair complexion.

"The eggs, darlin'. Mammy C always says 'tis better have a poke than try to juggle things in your hands."

"I expect Mammy C is right," he said. Now that he saw her in daylight, he realised she was older than he'd thought when she served him the night before, maybe close to his age. He indicated the geese with his chin because his hands were full. "This is going to sound odd, but do you see these geese?"

Her eyes danced with fun. "Sure I do. Six o' them. Plain as the handsome nose on your face. Why do you ask?"

"I wondered if I was hallucinating."

"Not a bit of it. Mind, they're fay geese, so they might be playin' a glamour on some folk here."

"They're playing something all right. Do you know how I can get them to stop herding me about?"

"You might get me grandad-by-love-but-not-by-blood to call 'em off. They're his geese. In the manner of speaking."

He sighed. "Look — um —"

"Cèilidh Acushla, darlin'. Me da-by-blood is Oison Seekjoy an' me da-by-love and a little by-blood is Alexander Peckerdale. Me mammy-by — "

He saw she was going to run through her whole pedigree

and said, "Please stop that. I take it you are related to the folk at the *Over Here B&B*?"

"I am that. Uncle Kris—that's me uncle-by-love and a little by-blood—is Daddy Alex's brother, and—"

He held up his eggs. "Can you call these geese off?"

She shook her head slowly.

"Would you hold these eggs and lend me your phone so I can call your uncle or your grandad to come and call them off?"

She turned out her hands in apology. "I don't have a phone. No manner o' use to me where I live." She put her head on one side, biting her lip. She seemed to find him amusing. "I can get ye a poke for the eggs though."

Poke? Ah, that was an old-fashioned term for a bag. *Pig in a poke*.

He waited for her to conjure one. Instead, she stepped up to a stall, chose two apples and put them into a paper produce bag. She held out money. The vendor shook his head and tapped his cheek. Cèilidh kissed him and then returned to Dequan. She took out an apple and bit into it. Then she handed him the bag with the other apple. "Love-gift for ye. *No harm*."

He glanced at the vendor, who winked back.

"Thank you," he said to both of them and loaded the eggs into the bag. By then there were four.

"Have you any idea where these geese want me to go?" he asked.

"Ye'll know when ye get there," she said logically.

"One more thing, Cèilidh."

She gazed up at him with sparkling eyes. She smelled pleasantly of pears. "Ask then, man."

"You were talking to a tall woman carrying baskets. What's her name?"

"Why do you want to know?" She sounded serious.

Dequan bent to pick up a fifth egg and put it in the bag. Luckily, the paper was of an industrial strength. "On Christmas night, I was talking to my ex-girlfriend. She said I should know what I want and put myself in the way of it. There's a woman I've started dreaming of. I call her the *fräulein*, but she's no one I've ever met. I think she's what I want, and I want to put myself in the way of her."

Comprehension shone from her face. "And now you see your heart's love in Martina."

"Maybe. If that woman with the baskets is called Martina. I don't know why I've suddenly started dreaming of her. I've never been here before."

Cèilidh said, "Well, darlin', I can tell ye that. 'tis the come-to-me." She reached out and touched the goose feather pin. It was a familiar gesture, but he knew Cèilidh was being helpful. She'd dropped the flirtatious air when she gave him the paper bag. "Just started wearin' this recently, right?"

"How did you know that?"

She shrugged. "Seems likely, if it's just started callin'. Fair keenin', it is."

"My grandmother gave it to me. She said her great-grandfather gave it to her, but she implied it was for luck."

"Luck, in the manner of speaking." She stroked it. "Bit particular, this one. It's a fay goose feather."

"Yes? Oh. Yes." He could have kicked himself for not making the connection between Gran's gift and his current dilemma before. "Do you think these geese want it back? Are they trying to trade eggs for it? I tried to unpin it last night, and it won't come off."

"I can't help ye, not bein' privy to the minds of fay geese." She stepped back and took another bite of her apple. "Best go wherever these blessed birds want ye to go."

"What about Martina?"

She seemed to debate with herself.

"I'm not going to pester her or anything. I promise. I'd just like to buy her coffee, maybe."

The dimple came back. "That's easy and no confidences broken. Martina runs a café called *Fee Kaffee*. Anyone might tell ye that if it's coffee you're wanting. Won't be open just yet a while, but when it is ye can order a drink and talk to her then."

"*Fee Kaffee.*"

"I see one of Uncle Kris' maps in your britches' pocket. You can find it on there."

He smiled at her with gratitude. She was being as helpful as she could be, without actively invading his *fräulein*'s privacy.

"Thank you, Cèilidh. I'll come back to the pub and tell you how I get on."

"I'm not working tonight. Going to take tay wid me brother-by-love-an'-a-little-by-blood an' his lovie. Sure, the love in those two has the birds singin' wid the joy of it."

He noticed her accent had thickened, but he said nothing of it.

Surprisingly, she got up on tiptoe and kissed his chin.

Just like Lucy!

He laughed.

"Road rise to ye, gooseman," Cèilidh said. She hesitated. "A Christmas wish on it? 'tis still the season."

"Why not?" Dequan said.

Cèilidh walked away.

Dequan looked down at the geese. They'd stopped hounding him while he conversed with the barmaid, but he had no illusions. "Let's go, then," he said to them.

Experimentally, he took a step back the way he'd come.

Hiss.

"Thought not." He turned and went the way they wanted.

CHAPTER ELEVEN: PHONE CALLS

Martina Bless, Fee Kaffee, December Twenty-seventh

Martina stared at the Christmas napkin with its brief message. Much as she longed to pretend one of the twins had doodled it in an idle moment, she knew better.

Her baker was missing.

The twins had eloped.

They can't have.

They can. They have.

Gott im Himmel!

Martina turned abruptly, leaving the bowl of eggs and flour unmixed. She conjured a hot cloth and wiped her hands, and then she returned through the connecting door to her rooms.

Back in her bedroom, she stared into the pier glass. Her troubled face stared back.

"This is not my fault," she said.

Nina will think it is.

She breathed on the glass and watched the mist settle over the surface. Once more, she thought of the twins.

A white feather hung in the glass.

Oh . . . it's my gentleman of the bedchamber . . .

She reached for the feather, but the glass cleared abruptly, leaving her staring at her reflection.

"A lot of help you are!" Martina swept out of the bedroom and returned to the café kitchen, where she continued mixing the egg-bread. Maybe Yannick's old van had broken down.

Maybe the twins had gone to the market. They could have zigged when she zagged.

Despite her early start, she was behindhand as she readied the café for opening. Usually, mornings ran with the precision of a cuckoo clock, with Yannick managing the baking while the girls did the marketing and then returned to help her lay tables, fix the flowers, and load the outdoor bird feeders.

Doggedly, Martina cleaned, prepared, arranged, and inventoried.

Some people wondered how she managed *Fee Kaffee* with only three permanent staff besides herself. The wonderers were humans, and indeed the casual human staff sometimes slowed things down. None of them could conjure, and most of them clashed with Yannick, who seemed to consider himself above the casuals.

Doing the work of four people, Martina wished she hadn't told *all* the casuals they could have the week off.

She shaped loaves, glazed them, and then she slid them into the oven.

She checked the inventory of cakes.

There would be enough left from yesterday's baking to serve today, but Yannick hadn't baked ahead. Where *was* the wretched young man? Was he really with the twins? It seemed so unlikely.

Martina dried her hands. Despite her earlier decision, she keyed in Lili's number.

Her niece's voice came brightly from the speaker. "Hey, this is Lili Bless. Leave a message."

"Lili, where are you? Where's Chiara? Is Yannick—"

Your message is being converted into text.

Right . . . Chiara.

"Chiara here. If you're after Lili, you have the wrong number. If you really want me, it depends on what you want—"

"Chiara, where are you? Are you all right? Your mother is—"

Your message is being converted into text.

Martina showed her teeth and hit Yannick's number. She knew it was no use. He never did answer his phone.

"Yannick."

"Really? Where are you? Do you know where the twins have got—"

Your message is being converted into text.

"Grrrr," Martina said.

Her phone rang.

Nina.

She sighed. "Hello again, Nina."

"I thought I asked you to get the twins to call me when they got in."

"They haven't got in yet. It's not even eight o'clock."

"Have them ring me."

Nina hung up.

Martina blew out her cheeks.

She hit contacts so hard the phone squawked in protest. "Call Florien."

Calling Florien.

Martina gritted her teeth. *I will not criticise Nina to my brother.*

"Martina? Has Nina rung you?"

"Yes. Twice."

"You know, then."

"Know what?"

"Didn't she tell you?"

"Flor, get on with it!"

"All right, don't chuck a spaz. Look, the twins are missing. And please don't say *twins*, or *missing*, with or without a question mark. I take it they're not with you."

"I haven't seen them since they clocked off last night at six," she said truthfully.

"Did they say where they were going?"

"They just said *Gute Nacht Tante* in two-part harmony."

"No need to take the piss."

"I'm not. They usually do say that."

"What else did they say?"

"They yelled out *Gute Nacht kleiner Bruder* to Yannick, and that's the last I saw of them."

"They said what to who?"

Whom.

"Yannick Langel. My baker."

"Why were they talking to your baker? Isn't he a bit peculiar?"

She winced. *Must you say that? He's not peculiar. He's . . . unusual.* There was no point getting into that now, though, so she said, "I have no idea why. It's not as if they could expect an answer." She drew in a deep breath. "I haven't seen them since then. Have you asked Luca?"

"Nina has. He says he doesn't know where they are."

"Well, as I already told Nina, twice, and you, once, they're not here." She hesitated. "You've checked with Dario, and with the hospital?"

"Dario's still in Melbourne, and if they'd been in an accident, someone would have said. Or they would have let us know. Besides, their bikes are here."

"They're twenty."

"What's your point?"

Martina shrugged. "They're adults. They've had enough years to be emancipated by either fay *or* human mores for over two years now."

"So they don't owe Nina and me an explanation for not bothering to come home, or for coming home and leaving again without a word to us?"

"Not really. It's surprising they haven't moved out by now. Since they haven't, I allow they might with courtesy let you know if they were planning not to come home."

There was a pause. He said, "I want your word on it that

you don't know where they are and had no hand in this."

She felt the small surge of a compulsion. Nevertheless, she said evenly, "You have my assurance. I haven't seen the twins since they left here yesterday evening. I had no hand in this. I assumed they were going home."

"I want your assurance you will call Nina as soon —"

"No." Martina turned her head. Someone was banging on the door. "Don't call me again. Tell Nina if she pesters me about this, I will put a block on her number and a compulsion on her. No — not a word! You just did it to me on much less provocation. When I see the twins, I will tell them you called. I will *not* tell them to call. I will not call myself unless they ask me to. They're adults." She cut the connection and turned, with relief, to the café door.

I didn't tell a lie. I said I hadn't seen them, not that I hadn't heard from them.

In any case, what would Florien make of two words and a symbol inked on a Christmas napkin? It might not even be a message. It might be just a doodle, possibly made to annoy Yannick.

Where the hell is Yannick?

Time had got away during her marathon phone session. She ought to have opened up five minutes ago.

"No need to be so impatient," she muttered as the knocking resumed. She left the kitchen and stepped into the café. She tied on a clean apron and conjured the street door open.

"*Guten tag!* And likewise, good morning! What —" Her habitual speech of welcome broke off in a squawk of shock as a man and six geese swarmed into *Fee Kaffee.*

Chapter Twelve: The Gooseman Cometh

Martina Bless, Fee Kaffee, December Twenty-seventh

"*Gott im Himmel!*" Martina stared at the invaders.

The geese broke into a chorus of honks and hisses, flapping their wings and swirling about the man's knees.

"*Fräulein!*" He took an uncertain step towards her and tripped.

The sturdy brown bag he was holding shot out of his hands.

Martina hurriedly conjured it to the nearest table before she stepped forward to aid the gooseman from the market.

She'd wanted to talk with him, but she hadn't expected him to arrive at her café with all his geese.

"Get them out of here!" she said.

The gooseman had fallen heavily to one knee in a welter of geese. He seemed to be looking for his paper bag.

"It's over there," Martina yelled over the honks and flapping.

He tilted a hand in acknowledgment and got back to his feet. He retreated out of the café, but the geese redoubled their noise and bullied him back in again.

"Out!" Martina insisted.

He stepped out and went down again amid thrashing wings and darting bills.

Martina gave a huff of exasperation and stalked towards

him. She was still angry over the fuss with Florien and Nina. "Control your birds!"

"They're not my birds." His voice came out every bit as loud and exasperated as hers in the sudden silence as the geese ceased hostilities.

"*Not* your birds?"

"I don't have birds, and if I did, they wouldn't be geese." His voice shook as he got to his feet again and stood staring at her across three paces of floor.

"Then why have you brought them to my café? Is this an advertising stunt? Some prank?"

He turned out his hands. She noted they were good hands and that they were free of rings. He was half a head taller than her.

"I honestly don't know what to make of it, unless they want *this*." He indicated a white feather fixed to his linen shirt with a gold pin.

"Maybe you should let them have it," Martina suggested.

"I would, if I could get it off the shirt."

One of the geese ruffled up its feathers, squatted and laid an egg. Martina stared at it in fascination.

"They *will* keep doing that," the man said. He smiled suddenly. "They keep wanting me to take the eggs. Do you think you could use them?"

"Not on your life, gooseman."

"Don't you use eggs in your cakes?"

"Not from crazed geese." She made a shooing motion.

He backed away. Martina advanced, driving the gooseman and the geese slowly out of her café.

Eventually, they all stood on the footpath outside.

Martina sighed. Now that all was quiet, she made another attempt to elicit information.

"I saw you at the market," she said.

"I saw you, too, but I couldn't get a look at your face. I

asked someone about you, and she . . . that person . . . said your name is Martina and you run this café." He waved at the closed door.

"Who did you ask about me, and why? Was it Cèilidh Acushla? I was talking to her just after I saw you."

He bit his bottom lip.

"I don't mind if she directed you to *Fee Kaffee*. It's open to the public, and my name is no secret. Cèilidh's a friend. It's okay, except for the geese."

He looked relieved. "She didn't say anything personal, just that I could get a cup of coffee once you were open."

"I don't see why you brought the geese."

"I didn't. They brought me."

"Well, I'm officially open for business. Or I will be when I get a chance to put the sign out. Come in but leave your geese outside."

CHAPTER THIRTEEN: MOCHA

Dequan Qin, Fee Kaffee, December Twenty-seventh

Now he'd met Martina, Dequan was certain that she was the living embodiment of his *fräulein*.

She stepped back towards the door and opened it a quarter way.

"Come in, gooseman. Just you, not the geese."

He was prepared for them to swarm after him as soon as he abandoned them. To his bemusement they settled on the pavement, squatting in the morning sunlight and preening their crisp feathers with the sound of someone running a thumb across a sheaf of playing cards.

The relief of being goose-free was indescribable and he sat down at one of the tables in the charmingly appointed café.

Martina remained standing. She was a metre away, but he smelled her signature scent, or what Gran Qin called *le bouquet de fees*. It reminded him of slightly bitter chocolate mixed with coffee and he breathed it in rapturously. *Essence of fräulein.*

"What would you like?" she asked.

Dequan wanted to say, *You, preferably naked in a feather bed and licking my balls.* He restrained himself. It *was* her, but he'd already strained the friendship via the geese invasion. Besides, he'd promised the barmaid that he'd not be a pest.

"I'd like mocha without sugar or marshmallow."

"Coming up." She gave him a professional smile.

Dequan looked at the white tables spread with checked

cloths. There were paintings on the walls, and he recognised the alp artist's style. These showed scenes from the café, and he thought the patrons depicted were real portraits. He got up to look, studying each in turn.

Martina featured in many, holding an order pad, watering flowers, and sitting on a low wall with her arms around two much younger women. They all had their ankles crossed and they were laughing. Behind them, in the shadows, stood a dark-haired man with an averted face.

"That was done three years ago when we opened," Martina said from behind him. "My nieces, Lili and Chiara."

"Who's the demon king?"

"That's Yannick, my baker. He doesn't come out in photographs, so we had to resort to painting."

He smiled, hoping it was a joke. Fairies were real. That didn't mean he had to believe in vampires.

Martina set down a tray bearing tall glasses with handles and some bread and butter. "The artist is Kristos Peckerdale. He's a local — owns the gallery near the B&B."

"I've met him, and I have one of his maps." Dequan went on staring at the painting. He would rather look at the real Martina, but he was afraid of saying something inappropriate.

She moved to sit and waved him back to the table.

"You're joining me?" His heart did a glad skip.

"There's no one else here at present, but I'll have to get up if someone comes in. For some reason, my entire staff is MIA. Demon king included."

He sat down and picked up his drink. It tasted the way she smelled.

Martina sipped hers and looked him over with a crease between her brows. "You said . . . implied . . . you wanted to talk to me," she said.

"I do."

"And?"

He looked into her clear grey eyes and decided he owed her the truth. Some of it, anyway. The respectable, non-pestering part.

"I'm here on a mystery holiday." He explained about his voucher, skipping the complicated genesis of the thing.

"I understand. I provided some of the chits you have for use while you're here."

She sipped her drink again and pushed the plate of bread towards him. "Try some *eierbrot*. Properly, it's an Easter dish, but since my baker failed to arrive, I made this in a hurry. It's supposed to be made with goose eggs, but—"

He said, reproachfully, "I just offered you goose eggs. I had some in a paper bag." He looked about and spotted the bag on one of the empty tables. "You turned them down."

"I was discourteous. Do go on, though."

He took a bite of the stuff she called *eierbrot,* which tasted like an enriched rye bread. "It's good."

"Better with goose eggs. I know, I know . . . and I shall graciously accept those eggs after all, if they're still on offer. You were saying?"

He described how the V-S car had arrived so early on Boxing Day morning, and how he'd ended up still in the shirt he'd worn on Christmas Day.

"That's why I have this on," he said, indicating the feather pin. He explained its sketchy provenance.

"Cèilidh said it was a come-to-me. Does that make sense to you?"

"My people don't use them much. The leppies do. So do some others."

"Are you German? I've been thinking of you as German." She said, "No. I'm alpenfee."

He supposed he looked blank, for she said, "Alpenfolk. I'm an alpmaid. A *mädchen*. No?"

He shook his head.

"Fairy? Fay? Fee?"

"Yes, I get that. The old man who gave the thing to Gran Qin was a courtfolk man, and he was my great-great- or great-great-great-"

"Never mind the generations. It's confusing . . . unless one is a leppy."

"Not German, then," he said.

"Not in the least. However, some of my ancestors probably came from Switzerland in the days when there was less of a divide between my people and the humans near the gates." She gave him a quizzical look. "You seem disappointed. Why did you want me to be German?"

"This will sound odd."

"And turning up in my café pursued by geese is not odd?"

"Odder. I dreamed of you on Christmas night, and then a couple of times since."

"We'd never met until today. I would have remembered," she said.

"I know. But I dreamed of you. For some reason, I thought you were German. I've been calling you *the fräulein*."

"I suppose it's a fair enough mistake. The *mädchen* would be more accurate, if you wanted to give me a generic title. You don't need to do that now. You can think of me as Martina if you think of me at all."

"Martina what?"

"Martina Bless."

"It suits you."

"Thank you. And your name?"

"Didn't I tell you?"

"Not yet. I've been thinking of you as the gooseman."

"Dequan Qin," he said.

She pursed her lips. "I wouldn't have expected that, although I don't know what I *did* expect. When I saw you at the market, I was trying to work out what order you are. Possibly kanaal fee. I wouldn't have said courtfolk."

"I'm not . . . well, aside from my great-great-great."

"What's your other blood?"

"Pure human. Mum's parents were born in the Netherlands and Dad's people came from China during the gold rush, invested in property, and stayed."

She nodded, assessing him. "That explains it, then."

He waited, but she didn't tell him what it explained.

She said abruptly, "Do you feel like telling me what I was doing in your dreams?"

"Not really."

"Then our business is probably finished, which is a pity," she said.

The café door opened and a group of four women came in. Martina got up unhurriedly and went to seat them. "Good morning and welcome. Are you ready to order?"

"Not yet." One of the group reached for a menu.

Another said, "Did you know there's a flock of geese on the footpath?"

"I was hoping they'd gone," Martina said. "They didn't bother you?"

"No, they're sitting so quietly I thought they were Christmas figurines until one of them moved."

"Christmas?" Martina sounded taken aback.

"You know . . . as in six geese a laying. I was looking for a partridge in a pear tree."

"I see. Let me know when you're ready to order."

"We will."

One of the younger women said, "Is this where Chiara Bless works?"

"It is, but she's not in today."

Martina returned to Dequan's table.

He said, "Chiara is one of your MIA staff?"

"Yes, one of the twins in the painting. My niece." She looked down at him. "Can I get you anything else?"

"No—why did you ask about my dreams?"

"I was trying to work out why you should dream of me. I thought the context might be helpful. Dreams generally come from the subconscious trying to make sense of material gathered from the conscious world."

"Generally?" he said.

She lifted one smooth shoulder. "Except when they don't. I wondered if you have been in the café sometime, maybe during the *Counterpoint* festival. You might have seen me without knowing who I was."

"I've never been in Patterdale before. Do you spend time in Sydney?"

"I have relatives there, but we generally meet up elsewhere. Maybe you know one of the Hallers. I don't know that any of them look like me, except as a general type."

"Do they smell of mocha?"

"Maybe. I don't know them all."

"It's you, though."

"Maybe you dreamed of someone else, and somehow your mind conflated that person's image with mine."

"It was *you*. In every detail."

"Even my clothing?"

"Maybe not quite that."

She looked at him thoughtfully. "If this was a romance, you might say you saw me *in dishabille* in that dream and were enchanted by an edelweiss marked out on my lower back. I would turn my back and slowly roll up my blouse to reveal that self-same edelweiss."

He found he was picturing that scene. It made him feel uncomfortable.

"I didn't see your lower back," he said in a stifled voice.

Martina smiled. "It wouldn't have proved anything. I have

no identifying marks to offer."

"Excuse me, waitress!" someone from the other table called. "We're ready to order now."

Martina turned away. "What would you like to have?"

Chapter Fourteen: Table Service

Dequan Qin, Fee Kaffee, December Twenty-seventh

Dequan hoped Martina would return when she'd finished serving the other table, but by then, more people had entered the café.

He watched with growing unease as she served three more tables, all of whom commented on the geese on the pavement.

By ten o'clock, he was still there. The geese were outside. Martina was inside. No contest.

The café was loud with conversation, and some of the patrons were restive.

One man got up and walked out, saying audibly, "Sorry, but I can't wait. Does it always take so long to be served?"

"I'm short-staffed today," Martina said.

"Then I suggest you hire more staff. There's no point saving money on wages if people walk out and complain to their friends, now is there?"

"No indeed, sir." Martina turned her attention to a party of five.

"We'd like coffee to go," one of them said. "We're pushed for time."

"I'll have it ready in a moment."

Dequan saw three young women staring him down. "Yes?"

"You've finished. Would you mind moving?" one said.

"There are three empty seats. I'm willing to share."

The women conferred, and two of them glanced at the

door.

Dequan accepted defeat. He picked up his glass and Martina's and put the last piece of bread in his mouth. Munching, he carried the crockery through into what he presumed was the kitchen.

Martina was assembling takeaway coffee.

Dequan noted the washing up was piling in the double sink, and he went over and filled one side with hot water. He rolled up his sleeves and set to work.

Martina took the coffees out and then returned with a tray. She gave Dequan a startled look.

He waved a wet tea towel. "Any more of these, *fräulein?*"

She clicked her fingers and a pile of dry ones appeared.

Dequan changed the rinsing water and returned to the crockery mountain.

Five minutes later, an order pad plopped on the draining board.

Eierbrot with cheese and cider for two- Table 16.

"Okay," he said.

The *eierbrot* was the bread she'd served him. There were loaves of it covered with a muslin cloth in the larder. The cheese was presumably the large wheel of openwork swiss on the board beside it.

"Butter?"

"Blue crock," Martina called.

He made curls of butter and put them in a dish, piled up the bread and cheese and added washed celery he found standing in ice water.

Table sixteen. Bearing the order on a wooden platter, he located the table and slid it onto the cloth.

"Thanks," one of the patrons said.

The other said, "You forgot the cider."

"Just coming, sir." He returned to the kitchen and located a jug of cider and some tankards, picked up a silver butter knife and a small dish of figs and added them to the order.

He had returned to the crockery mountain when another paper popped into sight.

Light salad for one –no cheese-no onion. Table 2.

Lettuce, tomatoes, baby carrots . . . he found salad dressing in the larder and put some in a miniature jug.

"Bread, ma'am?"

"Oh . . . yes, please."

He set down a ready prepared plate and a glass of water he'd decorated with a slice of lemon.

Alpenkuchen and black coffee for two. Table 7.

Coffee was easy, but what the hell was *alpenkuchen?*

He thought *kuchen* was German for *cake,* and presumably, the *alpen* bit referred to snow or an alp? A chocolate cake with thick white icing and cream might fit the description.

The time sped by until two o'clock, which brought a lull.

Martina came into the kitchen. "We usually do scones with jam and cream and fruit platters at three, but Yannick didn't make the scones and I didn't have time."

"I can make plain scones."

"Use the electric oven. Flour's in the crock over there, milk and buttermilk in the larder, butter —"

"I know where things are. How many?"

"Say fifty? Can you manage that?"

"Yes. I'll use those goose eggs."

She flicked her fingers and the bag of eggs appeared in front of him.

"By the way, I ate half the apple," she said.

"That's fine. It was a freebie anyway. It came along with the bag."

"The other half is —" It arrived on the board in front of him.

"Thank you!"

He ate it as he did quick sums in his head, halving the number of eggs, on account of their size. He turned on the electric oven and set to work.

While the first batch baked, he made up glass bowls of

different coloured jam and whipped cream.

He was slicing oranges when Martina came in. "Leave the peel on, and there's lemon juice—"

"—to spray over the apple and pear slices. Got it."

She refilled the urn. "I'm closing at five today," she said over her shoulder.

He took that to mean he'd better hurry with the fruit.

Martina wrote the closing time on a chalkboard easel. "Do you mind?"

He went to set it by the door. It was a shock to see the six geese there, impersonating statues. Three more eggs sat among them, so Dequan scooped them up. "Geese a laying. Shouldn't you lot be getting back to your cranky owner?"

The geese ignored that.

He went back in.

"The geese are still there," he told Martina.

"So I hear, from every new customer. I think some people are coming just to look at them."

At five, Martina served the last tables and hung the *closed* sign on the door.

Dequan cleared tables and did a final round of washing up. He removed soiled cloths from the table and towel rails.

The last people left, and Martina conjured the cloths somewhere, presumably to wash. He hadn't spotted a dishwasher, but he assumed she had a washing machine . . . unless she used a boiling copper and a copper stick. He wouldn't put it past her.

She went about, putting things to rights and clearing the larder, and then she quietly made a pot of tea.

"We've earned this," she said.

Dequan sipped his in between bites of sandwiches he'd made with leftover Christmas ham and mustard.

When he'd finished, Martina said, "Do you feel like telling me about those dreams?"

"Not really." He fished the book of chits out of his pocket and paged through it. "*Fee Kaffee,*" he said, and tore one out.

Martina laughed. "Let's forget that today. In fact, you've earned the right to eat lunch here for the rest of your stay. If you want to, that is."

He wanted to, but he smiled and returned the booklet to his pocket. "I ought to get back to the B&B."

Martina rose and offered her hand. "Thank you, goose-man."

"Thank *you, fräulein.*" He hesitated before he took her hand, raised it to his lips and kissed it.

She said, "That was an interesting experience."

"Having your hand kissed? I'd have thought you'd be used to that."

"I am, but I meant the whole day, geese and all."

This seemed to be that, so he moved reluctantly to the door.

He tried to look forward to another night in the alp room and more exploration of Patterdale tomorrow, but he could think of much nicer things to do.

Ask her, then. She can say no.

You promised that nice barmaid you wouldn't be a pest.

He let himself out.

The geese were still there.

"Don't you lot have somewhere to be?" he said.

He glanced along the footpath, orienting on the way back to the B&B. He'd come via the market, but the B&B should be a few streets along from the café.

He got five paces from the door before the geese erupted from their somnolent poses and set up a chorus of honks and hisses.

Another pace brought a good wing beating about the shins, and some angry pecks.

Not again!

He wheeled and returned to the door. The geese crowded about his heels and squatted there while he knocked on the door.

No answer.

He knocked again. "Martina!"

Silence.

He filled his lungs and hollered, "Martina!"

After thirty seconds, she opened the door. "Yes?"

Dequan indicated the geese. "They won't let me leave."

"Oh, for pity's sake."

"I'll show you." He stepped over two geese and the whole lot boiled up in an instant.

Martina backed away. "Can you slide in without letting those vicious-beaked Visigoths back into my clean café?"

"Just watch me."

He slid through the door. It clicked shut behind him.

"Is there another way out?"

She said, "Yes. I live in the attached house. There's a second entrance onto the street through my garden. I'll let you through that way."

"Okay."

She gave him an odd look. "Whatever did you do to those geese to get them into this state?"

"Nothing. They just took it in their heads to chase me about. I hoped they'd get bored and leave once I got into the café."

Martina conjured open a door. "This way. Straight through."

He walked through a delightful little house that seemed familiar. He realised it was furnished in a similar style to his room at the B&B, though it lacked the *trompe l'oeil* alp. It also matched the chalet of his dream *fräulein*.

He wondered if Martina had a feather bed with a Christmas coverlet.

She didn't give him time to go sight-seeing. She indicated a door at the end of a corridor. "That leads out into my back garden and then to the street. Turn right and go three blocks. Turn right, and one block should take you to the B&B."

"Thanks." He took her hand again. "This is surreal."

She opened the door and indicated that he should leave *quietly*.

"I wonder how long it will be before your escort realises you've given them the slip," she said in a low voice as he stepped into the small garden.

Dequan crept down the path. He was about to open the gate when it swung open by itself. He glanced back. Martina must have conjured it.

She waved.

He waved back and stepped out.

This time, he got ten paces along the pavement before a clap of wings made him duck and fling up his arms to protect his head.

The geese were on him again, and they were angry.

"Bloody hell!" He turned and sprinted back to the gate. "Martina!"

She let him in. The geese crowded into the garden.

Martina grabbed his arm and hauled him into her cottage. "This is getting scary."

"I know," he said, rubbing his leg where a wing had whopped him. "I left my phone at the B&B, so will you call Kris for me? They take notice of him."

"I could, but . . ." She stared at him and indicated the goose feather pin. "Remember your interesting theory about that?"

"I was joking."

"No joke. If that thing's responsible, I suggest you take it off and let them have it."

"Gran Qin gave it to me."

"I don't think your grandmother wants you to be chased up hill and down dale by six homicidal geese, do you?"

"Probably not," he admitted. *Aunt Cherie might.* There was a novel thought.

"Right, then. Take it off."

Dequan tried to remove the pin, but again he couldn't come to grips with it. "Martina?"

She huffed, tucked a stray lock of hair into her braid, and took hold of the pin in a *this is the way you do it* manner.

She fiddled for a bit. "Sorry. You'd better take the shirt off."

"What? Here?"

"Don't be silly. I've certainly seen a few bare chests. I have brothers."

"Yes, but . . ."

"Arms out."

He grabbed protectively at his buttons, and she batted his hands away. Then she unbuttoned him. "Get it off and hand it over."

Awestruck, he did so. Martina carried the shirt into a small and beautiful sitting room and turned on a goose-necked lamp. She worked on the pin for three long minutes. Then she handed it back with a shrug.

"Sorry, gooseman. I can't undo it. We could snip it off. Or you can give them the whole shirt."

"It's the only one I've got! I was going shopping this morning."

"I'll lend you one of my brother's. He owes me."

Reluctantly, he wadded up the shirt with the feather pin on the outside. "Here goes, then." He walked to the back door, opened it a slit and peeped out.

Twelve alert orange eyes swivelled in his direction. The geese had settled on the porch like fat angels.

"Come and get it." Dequan bundled the shirt out the door.

Martina nodded approvingly. "Let's have coffee, and then I'll get that shirt from Florien and you can leave by the café gate."

Chapter Fifteen: The Shirt

Martina, Fee Kaffee Chalet, December Twenty-seventh

Martina was having a trying day, but the gooseman was a good distraction from her family troubles.

She made coffee in her kitchen and brought it into her sitting room.

Having a shirtless stranger in the house was a novel experience, but he seemed uneasy.

"I'll borrow that shirt now. It will be an old one, since I can take only what Florien would give me without a second thought."

And what Nina won't question him about.

Dequan cocked an eyebrow at her.

"You understand conjuring?"

"Sort of. I can't do it, but for people who can, things just pop into view. I think there are limits on what you can conjure."

"Yes, conjuring is limited to what we own or could practically or ethically acquire elsewise. What *do* you do, gooseman? Aside from not-conjuring, helping out in cafes and enraging geese?"

"I locate things. I find staff and I curate collections. Basically, I do what other people could do for themselves, but I do it faster and more efficiently. Something like conjuring."

"Tell me three things you've located for clients."

"Shirt," he said.

"What?"

"Please, may I have that shirt?"

"Oh, all right."

Pity, I was enjoying the view.

She focused on her brother Florien's closet, and she selected a shirt that was a close cousin to the one they'd donated to the geese.

Dequan squawked with shock as the shirt assembled itself around his torso.

"Perfect fit." Martina chuckled at his expression. "That was discourteous, but I wanted to see if I could still dress someone else remotely. I stopped being able to do it for my nephew when he turned six and his mother deemed it inappropriate." She caught herself up, not wanting to think of Nina. "You were about to tell me three things you've located for clients."

"I found an apostle spoon for a woman's collection. Sixteenth Century Saint Paul in silver. She wanted to complete her set. Last week, I found agistment for a family's pony that *wasn't* two hours away by train, which was the nearest the family had managed to find. I—" He broke off.

"Tell me."

"Okay, this might shock you, but I found a sex tutor for my cousin. He's an elf man—mostly—and I've known him off and on for years. I wouldn't have felt right setting her up with someone I didn't know."

"You trusted him not to get a baby on her or upset her in any way."

"Yes. I told him I'd have his nuts for a Waldorf salad if he messed her about." He smiled and added, "that was a freebie. Otto didn't want payment for his services, so I did it pro bono. Generally, I have a scale of charges based on the difficulty of the job and the value to the customer."

"Did the tutor give satisfaction?"

"Oh, yes. My cousin still refers to him as *darling Otto*, although they were never a couple. I don't know why not, since they hit it off so well."

"I expect I could tell you why not," Martina said.

"Oh?"

"Precisely *because* she thinks of him as *darling Otto*. She probably wanted to keep him as a perfect memory that could never be tarnished."

Dequan's eyes lit up. "That's Lucy all over! She knows what she wants."

Martina saw the affectionate expression in his eyes and thought his cousin was a lucky woman. She found herself comparing Dequan's apparent love for this Lucy and Florien's mild affection for her. He'd even put a compulsion on her in regards to the twins and their whereabouts.

She said, "I suppose your occupation explains why you slotted in so neatly as my temporary staff. Thank you for that, by the way."

He laughed. "I've served my time as a kitchen hand and wait staff. My mother brought me up to be domesticated and instilled an annoying work ethic in me. I couldn't just sit by and let you be snowed under."

Her opinion of him rose a notch.

"Do you feel like telling me about those dreams?"

His smile faded. "I ought to be going. I don't know if there's a curfew at the B&B, but I need to get dinner sorted. And no, I'm not angling for you to feed me. I enjoyed my day, apart from the geese, but I'm sure you have things to do." He got up. "The departure of Dequan, take three."

"Café door or street door?" Martina asked.

"Café door. The geese are lying in wait in your garden."

"Not now, I trust. Oh." A twinge of *the sight* had just informed her the geese were still there.

"Café door," she agreed.

He took her hand. "Thank you for offering me sanctuary. I'll go shopping tomorrow and get your brother's shirt laundered at the B&B. I'll drop it back to the café sometime this week."

"Thank you."

She saw him through the café and let him out. She'd barely made it back to the dividing door when she heard an anguished yelp and subsequent agitated knocking on the door.

"Martina!"

"Coming." She let him in and shut the door on six indignant bills. "No dice?" she said with sympathy. She raised her brows and bit her lip, trying not to smile. He looked so ruffled, and he'd evidently trodden on an egg.

"*Verdomme die ganzen naar de hel!*" he snarled.

"Oh, dear, oh, dear," Martina said. "Shall I conjure you a shotgun?"

He stared at her. Then he laughed. "You couldn't. I wouldn't."

"Indeed. *Ganzen* means geese, I take it?"

"It's Dutch," he said.

"I think I can guess the rest."

They eyed one another.

"The feather didn't appease them."

"No."

"And you really have no idea why they're doing this."

He turned out his hands. "None. I thought it had to do with Gran's present, but as you say, it didn't appease them."

"Would you like to call your grandmother?"

"I would if I thought she could help, but I'm sure she doesn't know any more about the thing than she told me. Besides, I don't have it now. They have it, and they're still in attack mode. I would like to call Kris Peckerdale at the B&B though. He got them off my case yesterday."

"We'll call him, then. I have his direct number in my contacts."

Martina conjured her phone. "You might as well take your shoes off and come through into the sitting room."

Silently, he took off his shoes. Then he walked barefoot through the café, located a floorcloth and cleaned the egg off the tiles.

Martina's opinion rose again.

Back in the sitting room, she connected with Kris Peckerdale's number and put the phone on speaker.

"*Thymelines Gallery.* This is Richenda."

She offered the phone to Dequan, but he gestured for her to carry the conversation.

She nodded to him and said, "Greet you, Richenda. This is Martina Bless. Is Master Peckerdale there?"

"Which one?"

"Kris."

"No. Corin's here, but he's a bit tied up at the moment."

"Oh, dear. Be gentle with him."

"No. Why? He owes me a forfeit."

Martina tsked. "Richenda, is Master Peter there?"

"I do hope not."

"When you're finished torturing Corin, would you please tell Kris that I have his Vouch-Safe guest here and that there's a problem with geese."

"I will. *Nos da.*"

"*Nacht.*" Martina ended the call.

"Who was that?" Dequan asked.

"That was Mistress Richenda Pendennis. She's betrothed to Corin Peckerdale. Have you met Corin?"

"Yes. He gave me a magnifying glass. He smells of figs."

"Indeed, he does. No wonder Richenda can't keep her hands off him."

"Is she really torturing him?"

"Possibly, but you may be sure it's fully consensual. Anyway, as you no doubt heard, Kris is not there. Since he's left his phone behind, it's likely he's out of contact. Probably gone *over there.*"

"Is the local gateway close by?" Dequan asked.

85

"Not far, but I doubt if you'd get there with those geese in pursuit."

"So, what do I do?" He looked comically dismayed.

"I think the best, and possibly the only, sensible option is for you to stay here with me until Kris gets the message. No doubt Corin would come when Richenda chooses to release him, but Kris is the man you need. He has a strong affinity with animals. Mostly it's cats, but he's also good with dogs, and you said he got the geese away from you yesterday. He's one of the very few folk I know who can shift animal focus."

"Obviously the effect didn't last. They came back."

"How long did your freedom last?"

"I asked about dinner. Calypso said they didn't serve it. She suggested the *Pride of Erin* pub, so I went there."

"Unattended by geese?"

"Not a feather in sight."

"Other than the one on your shirt."

"Other than that—wait!" He held up a finger. "I just remembered! I left the shirt in the B&B when I went to dinner last night."

She gave him a quizzical look. "You said you hadn't got another one. The *Pride of Erin* is surprisingly liberal, but they might draw the line at bare-chested men in the public dining room."

"I put my jacket on. But that feather can't really be responsible. After all, I just went out now without it and got chased back in."

Martina got up. "I think you'd better resign yourself to spending the night here."

She waited for an acknowledgment of her oblique suggestion.

When he was silent, she looked up to find him looking troubled.

"What is it?"

"Martina, couldn't you drive me back to the B&B? I'd have to run the gauntlet from the gate to the B&B, but I'd be off your hands."

"I'd rather not do that."

He looked dashed, so she clarified, "I don't want to drive through the streets with six geese flying madly after us like the Ride of the Valkyries. They might cause an accident. I also prefer not to make a spectacle of myself. I live and work here and I like to think I'm well-respected."

"I see that."

She looked at him thoughtfully. "And besides, I've decided I don't want you off my hands. I'd like to spend the night with you, if you're not committed elsewhere and if you have no other objection."

Chapter Sixteen: Feather Bed

Dequan, Fee Kaffee Chalet, December Twenty-seventh

Dequan didn't pretend to misunderstand her offer. "I have no objection," he said.

Martina said, "I'm so glad. I'll enjoy you, and I hope you'll enjoy me, too. It's a bit early for supper, since we had those sandwiches, but I have to be up early in the morning."

"Will your staff be back tomorrow?" he asked.

"I don't know. They didn't give me any warning that they wouldn't be in today."

"Do they often do that?"

"Never before."

"Are they likely to be all right?"

"I trust they are, but they're out of contact. Their phones go to message bank and I can't conjure a note when I don't know where they are. They could send me one, but they chose not to."

He noted a tightening of her lips and saw she didn't want to discuss her missing staff with him. Fair enough.

"Maybe it's a good thing I'll be here in the morning. I can take up some of the slack."

"Thank you. Would you like supper now, or after?"

"After," he said.

"That's what I hoped you'd say." She put her phone on the small table and got to her feet. "My bedroom is through that door. Go up the stairs. There's a bathroom and a towel for you to use. I'll join you in a few minutes."

Dequan went through the door, which he'd taken to be a closet. The stairs were a tight open spiral, which made sense for such a small space. He found the bathroom, stripped and got into the shower. He was glad she'd suggested it. After a day of being chased about by geese and then working in the café, he felt sticky.

He was soaping up when he felt a sudden draught on his side, and he realised Martina had joined him.

"Ahhh," she said, arching her back. She held out her hand for the soap. "Turn around, gooseman."

He turned, and she applied the soap to his shoulders, and then lathered on down his back. Her touch was firm and decided. "Your turn," she said, and she stepped in front of him. He soaped her down, admiring her generous curves. She'd taken her hair out of its milkmaid braid and it hung in a rippling curtain down to her waist.

"That's enough." She took back the soap and rinsed off the suds before she stepped out of the shower and wrapped herself unhurriedly in a towel. He followed, watching with fascination as she pressed the water out of her long hair and then made a complicated gesture, leaving it almost dry.

"I didn't know you could do that," he said.

"Do what?" She arched her brows.

"Dry your hair that way." He rubbed his own with a towel. He ran a thumb over his chin. "I need a shave."

She stepped up and stroked his cheek. "I like it this way. I want a man in my bed, not a soft-cheeked lad. Are you ready?"

"I will be."

"Good. Come to the bedroom. May I have that towel?"

He handed it over.

She conjured both towels away and, without looking at him again, she moved from the bathroom to the landing and conjured open the opposite door.

Dequan looked at the tall looking glass, a dressing table, and an immense four-poster bed. It was piled with opulent looking pillows and covered with a patchwork quilt made from panels of solid colour, stitched with figures.

"Oh!"

Martina smiled at him. "That's my Twelve Days of Christmas coverlet. Not what you were expecting?"

"Well . . . you remember I said I'd dreamed of you? This was in the dream."

She conjured back the cover, revealing white linen sheets. "So this is why you wouldn't describe those dreams."

He laughed. "Yes. I promised Cèilidh I wouldn't bother you."

"We won't bother one another." She got into the bed and patted the mattress invitingly. "Have you ever had a woman in a feather bed?"

Dequan got in beside her. "I've never even *seen* a feather bed before. I didn't know they still existed, outside of my erotic dreams."

"You might find it a novel experience, then." She got up on her elbow and put her hand on his chest. "You usually use a condom?"

"Always, but I don't have any with me. I wasn't expecting this when I got up this morning."

"I wasn't expecting this either." She stroked his chest, tangling her fingers in the hair. "Have you ever had a fairy before?"

"I'm pretty sure I haven't."

"That makes us even then. I haven't had a human . . . a mostly human," she amended. "I enjoy courtfolk men most often, but as I grow older, my preference becomes more difficult to access."

"You can't possibly call yourself old."

"I'm probably around your age, but most courtfolk men

90

your age have been wed for a decade or more. While I've never insisted on exclusive bedding rights, I do take care not to *ever* take a man who owes his love and duty to someone else."

"I'm utterly single," he said. He turned over to face her. "Do you have condoms? I know Otto doesn't use them. He explained that when I asked him to tutor Lucy. He assured me there was no need. He said he'd make sure she understood that what was true for him was *not* true for humans. I'm mostly human."

Martina moved her hand to rest on his belly. "I'll take care of that aspect. You won't catch anything either. Nor will I. So—"

"So?" He put his hand over hers.

"I hope you'll relax so we can enjoy one another."

"I'm relaxed," he said.

She patted his hip. "I mean we'll put all trouble out of our minds. That means no geese, no family, no work, no regrets, no comparisons, and no thoughts of tomorrow."

"Definitely no geese." He held out his arms, and Martina let herself down into them. The mocha scent was all around him, as if someone had lit an expensive chocolate candle. He caught her mouth with his and kissed her. He was hard already.

Martina snuggled against him and said in his ear, "Relax and let go."

"I'm afraid of letting go too soon," he said, laughing. She'd been clear and straight-forward with him. He'd be the same with her.

"Oh, dear. That would never do." She squirmed down the bed, and he felt her long hair on his thighs. Her mouth . . .

Thoughts fell away as, for one perfect moment, his dream became his reality. He was in a feather bed with his *fräulein*, and her mouth was on his balls.

His toes curled and he gasped with pleasure until common sense snapped in. "Martina—I'm—"

She patted his thigh and lifted her head. "Let yourself go, *meine Liebe*." She laid her face down again and returned to her occupation. This time, she had a hand on his cock, stroking it from root to tip.

Well, she'd said to let go, so he took her at her word, releasing his control.

This is going to be messy . . .

It wasn't. Efficient as always, she'd got a soft cloth to catch the mess.

He was still gulping down shaken breaths when she came back up into his arms and kissed him. "Was this your dream?"

"Yes . . . But better."

"Now, I shall tell you about my gentleman of the bedchamber."

"No comparisons, remember?"

"My gentleman comes to me in dreams, but I never remember until he comes again. His visits go this way." She stroked his hair, drawing his head down against her breasts, so he felt every breath she took.

"I am lying in my bed, here, alone and naked. That's strange, because I generally wear a nightgown. The moonlight shines through my balcony window and I look up to see a feather coming down. Sometimes I see it as a swan feather, and I am happy because swans are together for life. Other times, it seems like an angel's. Possibly it might come from a goose."

"I thought we weren't thinking of geese," he said reproachfully.

"There are geese on my coverlet here. Geese are productive birds, and they warn of danger." She turned her face and kissed his head. "The feather, whatever it is, comes on down and then it dawns on me that this is my gentleman of the bed-chamber. I am *so* happy he's come to play with me again."

"How long has he been coming?" Dequan asked.

"It's so hard to say, because I never remember until he comes again."

"You're remembering now, though. Are you implying you're dreaming now, or that I'm dreaming of you?"

"Neither — but I think he came to prepare the way for us to be here together, just as your dream *fräulein* did."

Something stirred in Dequan's memory. "Did your gentle-man use that feather in any particular way?"

Martina's laugh gurgled up. "He does use it in a very par-ticular way."

"I wish I still had my feather," Dequan said, laughing, too.

"I, too, especially as the geese didn't want it," she said.

"Can you get it back for us?"

He felt her shoulder flex as she raised one shapely arm in a beckoning motion.

"Won't it come shirt and all?"

She laughed again. "I'm not risking that one, *meine Liebe*, in case it brings the geese along. I happen to have a feather I found this morning in my larder."

Dequan looked up in time to see a softly curved feather drifting down, just as Martina had described it. He held out his hand, feeling it land weightlessly in his palm. He got it between finger and thumb and got up on his elbow, so he was looking down into Martina's face.

"Does it matter that it's not moonlight, *fräulein*? We could wait."

Martin smiled up at him. "This is real."

"Yes." He waited a few seconds, before realising she wasn't planning to coach him.

"Is this a test?"

Her eyes widened. "No, my dear. Not at all."

He thought back to his latest dream. *Was that just this morning?*

Foreplay with feathers.

He traced her features gently with the feather, painting her in his memory.

Martina went on smiling, so he moved on down her shoulders and arms and then to her generous breasts. She caught her breath.

Ticklish? Something more?

He continued, aware of her dilating eyes. She was breathing heavily, and he said, "We can go on with this, or maybe—"

"Or," she said, between gasps.

He tucked the feather under the heaped pillows for safety and then rolled on top of her, filling her quickly.

Her gasp of satisfaction sounded authentic, and it excited him as she parted her legs and arched her back to receive him. Despite his earlier spill, his build-up was fast and relentless.

Trying to care for her needs, he began a catalogue in his mind.

First time in a feather bed, first time with a fairy woman, first time bare in any woman, first time for—

He felt her lungs inflate, pressing her breasts against him, and she arched higher, crying out on a long, melodious warble that broke his control.

He groaned, pumping hard, holding her hips as she bucked against him.

Breathless, he subsided and rolled off, still holding her so she gasped against his chest.

Certainly, it was the first time for *that.*

Somewhat shaken, he said, "Are you okay?"

She drew in more deep breaths and then sighed, giving his chest an open-mouthed kiss. She said tranquilly, "Of course, *meine Liebe.* Why would you think otherwise?"

"You were—" He broke off, unable to think of the words

to describe that extraordinary sound.

"I was what?" She stretched against him, her damp skin exuding that perfume that made him want to lick her all over.

"That sound."

She looked uncomprehending.

Dequan drew in a breath and tried to reproduce it.

"Oh!" She started to laugh, quivering in his arms, contriving to rub herself against him in a way he would have felt beguiling if he wasn't so confused.

The feather bed, deep, soft and generous, supported their bodies, and he felt a peculiar surge of emotion flow over him in a wave.

He smirked and then chortled, and then a gale of laughter shook him. He had no clear idea of what they were laughing about, but he felt sure she was all right.

He certainly was.

When he was laughed out, he shifted onto his back and rolled her up on top of him, looking up into her eyes.

In the dimming light, he saw her long eyelashes were spiked with tears of merriment.

"Well?" he said.

"Well—" She gasped and started laughing again before bringing her mouth down on his for a lingering and squelchy kiss.

His toes curled with delight and he rolled her over again so he had her trapped with an elbow on either side of her ribs.

"Now, my beautiful *fräulein*, explain yourself."

In answer, she rolled again.

"Stop that. You'll have us on the floor. No, don't start giggling again. You'll set me off."

She composed herself. "I'm sorry, *mein Gänsemann* but— ooh! Stop looking at me like that!"

He kissed her.

She sighed again. "You never had an alpmaid before."

"No, I told you that. Did I do something wrong? Against your custom?"

"You did everything splendidly, but I never had a human before and so—oh—I should have thought, but there was this one time when I had a courtfolk man. He was nineteen and so was I and he—oh, he was so *shocked* when I yodelled!"

Of course—that was the sound.

"I wasn't shocked—I just thought I'd hurt you."

"Not at all. I—" She gasped down a renewed attack of laughter and then said in a rush, "I-had-to-learn-to-be-silent."

"Really?"

"Not silent. No, but a few p-polite m-moans. It was so—"

"Yodel," he said thoughtfully. "You do that when you're having a good time?"

She patted his shoulder. "I was having a spectacular time . . ."

"Did I do the right thing with the feather? What your gentleman did?"

"You *are* the gentleman, but better, since you have a cock for me to play with and arms to hold me." She worked her hand down between them and stroked his cock. Then, she turned her face to add, "You're such a—*Gott im Himmel!*" She went rigid, staring over his shoulder as if she'd seen a ghost.

Dequan rolled over to look.

For a few seconds, his outraged eyes insisted they didn't see what he thought they saw. Twelve orange eyes gleamed through the window.

"What the fuck?"

"It's the geese," she said.

"Yes, but *how*?"

"They're on my balcony."

He swallowed. "How long do you think they've been there?"

"They weren't there when I conjured the feather."

Dequan stared at the geese. They stared back.

"Shoo! Go!" His arms tightened protectively around Martina. "This is going to sound peculiar."

"Everything's peculiar today," she said.

"Calypso at the B&B *and* Cèilidh from the pub both said these are fay geese. I don't understand what that means. Are they fairies? Gran said some fairies have unexpected shapes . . . sometimes."

Martina snuggled against him. "Undoubtedly. Calypso has, for one example."

"She looked normal to me."

Beautiful, naked, flexible, alluring . . . but normal.

"In her colleen form she does, although she's uncommonly supple, even for one of the green way folk."

"She has a different form?"

"I'm surprised you didn't meet her. Kris calls her Mistress Calico and wears her around his neck."

"The cat."

"Indeed. Pretty thing, isn't she?"

"No wonder I got the urge to inform her of what I was doing." He smiled, less surprised than he would have expected. "So, these Visigoths. Are *they* like that?"

"No."

"You sound certain."

"I am. If they were, we could reason with them. Fay geese, or fay goats, or fay cats or any other such things are animals originating *over there* or bred from *over there* stock. They're the same as human realm animals except that their characteristic attributes are intensified. They have a slight difference in appearance and more intelligence. Sometimes they are bigger, except for the fay cattle, which are smaller."

"Not the same at all, then," he said.

"Not so different."

"These geese are crazy. You said so yourself."

She kissed his throat.

"Martina, they're watching."

"Let them. I suspect they're under some kind of compulsion."

"And nothing to do with my feather, since they've got that." He added, plaintively, "Why would anyone in Patterdale want to set geese on me? They attacked as soon as I arrived. I didn't know anyone here. I didn't even know I was coming here. Almost no one knew I'd be here."

Martina kissed him again, with greater intent. "I would like to yodel again."

"I'd love to help you to yodel again, but we have an audience."

"Maybe we can shock them into going away. Relax." She fondled his cock.

He wanted to relax, but the twelve orange eyes seemed to be boring into him.

Martina huffed. She conjured the coverlet and sheet away and squirmed downwards.

Dequan, naked and exposed, jerked up his knees. "What are you doing, you mad *fräulein*? Oh!" His mouth dropped open as her tongue swiped his balls. "Martina!"

Incredibly, she giggled against him. "I want to yodel," she reminded in a muffled voice.

Her fingers pried his thighs apart and she went on licking and sucking.

Dequan's eyes, held by the mesmerising gaze of the six geese, blurred over. His toes curled in ecstasy. He hadn't had nearly enough of her administrations when she squirmed back up and sat on him.

That was even better.

He put his hands against her breasts, and she leaned in, with her flowing river of hair falling around them. He wondered dazedly where the feather was but there was no time to find it among the heaped pillows.

Martina executed a slow swivel. They gasped in unison,

and she flung back her head in a wild yodel.

Dequan's gasp turned into a laugh and he let go, with everything flowing in delight.

Martina slid down his body and uncoupled herself, before squirming into his arms. She, too, was shaking with laughter.

"*Gott im Himmel!*"

Dequan pulled her hard against him. His toes were still curling, and he felt supremely joyful.

Then he remembered the geese.

He turned apprehensively to the balcony window.

Moonlight poured in, uninterrupted.

"Martina, we must have traumatised them."

"Hm?" She turned to look.

"Oh." She unwound herself from him and climbed off the bed. She walked over to the balcony, opened the French door and, to Dequan's consternation, she stepped outside.

Moonlight turned her skin to pearl and shadow. She turned to look at him. "Come here, gooseman."

He looked about for his clothing, and then he remembered it was still in the bathroom.

"Quickly."

He got off the bed, walked over and, with a slight qualm, he stepped out beside her. "Are we likely to get arrested for disturbing the peace?"

She chuckled. "Not with the glamour I cast for us."

He relaxed. Standing naked in the moonlight was liberating. "Could I yodel you out here then?"

"No, *meine Liebe*. I am fully satisfied."

"May I—"

She tapped him on the cock. "Get your mind off this for a moment and observe." She indicated the balcony.

"The geese have gone."

"They've left us some eggs, but—"

"I suppose that means they're guarding the café door."

"No, *look.*"

He followed her outstretched arm and looked out over her garden and down the street. In the distance, he saw six geese, marching in formation.

"They're leaving?"

"I would say so."

His heart did a peculiar lurch. "So I don't need to stay the night."

"You do need to stay the night, and as many more as we can contrive."

"Oh, good. I don't think I could bear to go now," he said frankly.

He heard his words as if someone said them, but they felt true and frightening.

They watched the fay geese march out of sight. After that, they went for another shower. Martina changed the linen, and they ate supper in her sitting room before they retired to the feather bed.

This time, they slept.

CHAPTER SEVENTEEN: NEW YEAR'S EVE

Dequan, Patterdale, December Thirty-first

Thursday was New Year's Eve.

Dequan was supremely happy when he woke. As on every morning since arriving at *Fee Kaffee*, he was snuggled with Martina in her feather bed. The cuckoo clock struck five, and he spent a few sleepy and blissful minutes reflecting on the night before.

Then, Martina swung her legs out of the bed and headed for the bathroom with her long hair veiling her naked body.

Dequan went downstairs and stirred the stove to bring the kettle to a boil before assembling breakfast.

Martina joined him after a brief interval in her working clothing of a dirndl and blouse, and with her hair pinned up in that neat braid. His *fräulein* of the feather bed had become the café owner again, friendly, efficient, but slightly detached. He remembered her uninhibited yodels of the night before. These never failed to heighten his pleasure with the ripple of laughter when they made love. He'd even achieved his ambition to yodel her in the moonlight on her balcony. He'd kneeled before her with his face in her warm thighs while she gripped the balcony rail.

"You now *meine Liebe*," she'd gasped, and he assumed the same position while she kneeled before him in her turn.

It was so strange to remember that as they walked decorously to the market.

Dequan had his own shirt back. Martina had recovered it,

unmolested, from outside the door on Monday morning. The feather pin had allowed Martina to unclip it without fuss, and it now resided with the hen feather in a drawer near the bed, wrapped in a napkin Dequan had found in the larder.

It was a glorious morning, and they bought the usual supplies and some private ones for a celebration supper.

As usual, Martina conjured the marketing on to the café. They strolled back by a slightly different route.

Dequan saw a familiar building and realised they were near the *Thymelines Gallery*. That meant they were also near the B&B.

"Kris Peckerdale never showed up to sort out the geese," he said.

Martina stopped and a small frown marred her forehead. "No. That's odd. He's a conscientious man."

Dequan said, "We didn't need him, as it turned out. I should go to the B&B and cancel the message."

"You go, while I get the baking started," Martina said.

"Won't be long." Dequan turned towards the B&B and Martina continued on her way to the café.

He had just closed the B&B gate when a cacophony of honks erupted behind him.

He yelped and tore through the garden and up the mossy steps, a pace ahead of six vengeful bills. He got the door open and slid through just in time.

Tingling with shock, he walked up to reception. There was no one there.

"Hello? Kris? Calypso? Corin?" There must be other staff members, but they were the three he'd met.

He waited a while, but no one came.

On a whim, he climbed the stairs and let himself into the alp room. It was beautiful. Everything was just as he'd left it on Sunday morning, but he had no wish to sleep there again. He was gathering his belongings when he heard something scrabbling against the window. He turned sharply, just in time to see a furious goose lose its purchase on the narrow sill and fall. He dashed to the window, expecting to see the creature sprawled on the ground below. Instead, he saw it coasting down on outspread wings.

Another one took off, flapping mightily, and landed on the sill.

He stared into its angry orange gaze until it overbalanced and tumbled.

"This is bizarre!" he said helplessly. He unplugged his phone from the charger on the bedside table and swiped it open.

There were no missed calls, no texts and no messages.

Well, he'd planned to spend some time figuring himself out without distraction, but seriously — *no one* had called? No clients, even? He'd expect nothing from Lucy, but Gran Qin or Lotte might have pinged him to ask about his mystery holiday.

Yet — did Lotte even know? She'd left for her Dutch Christmas before Lucy came home and before he booked his trip. Gran Qin would tell her . . . but did Gran Qin know?

Lucy knew.

Lucy was happily fucking like bunnies with her fairy lover.

Dequan laughed aloud. He had his own fairy lover now. They didn't fuck like bunnies, but yodelling in the moonlight was just as much fun.

Dequan stuffed his phone into the depths of his holdall. Then he left the alp room and walked downstairs.

It was still quiet, except for a black and white cat purring on the first landing and two guests murmuring in one of the rooms.

He opened the door a cautious crack.

The geese were on guard on the steps. Evidently, they'd given up on the window.

He stared at them. They stared back.

"Are you going to terrorise me again?" he asked.

One goose shuffled her wings meaningfully.

"My *fräulein* is waiting, so do what your worst." He stepped out and over two geese and walked down the steps. The flock fell in behind and around him, behaving more like an escort than like an avenging horde. They murmured and honked quietly as they trailed him through the gate and down the streets towards *Fee Kaffee*.

He heard the ping of a text, and then another and another, but there was no time to check his phone. Martina was waiting.

Why are people suddenly pinging me now?

He reached the café and tapped smartly for admittance.

The door swung open and he stepped in smartly, closing the door in front of the orange bills.

"My escort's back. I wonder if we should try yodelling them away again," he said to Martina as he walked through the connecting door to the café.

"*Yodelling?*"

"Well, it worked that first night when we put on the show for—" He stopped, as his mind informed him it wasn't Martina who had spoken.

He looked up sharply, straight into two faces which were both strange and disturbingly familiar.

He cleared his throat.

The two young women, dressed alike in dirndls and aprons like the ones Martina wore, were not identical, but they were the same height and had similar features.

They looked the way Martina might have looked ten years before.

Dequan smiled and said, "Lili and Chiara, I assume."

"I'm Lili," one said. She had hair the same colour as Martina's and eyes a little bluer.

Her sister, who had lighter hair and greyer eyes, said,

"That makes me Chiara, and everyone says Lili first, which is odd since I come first alphabetically."

"I'm older, that's why," Lili said.

"Ten minutes."

"A day, technically. Anyway," Lili said.

"You must be Dequan," Chiara finished.

"You've been helping *Tante* Martina, and she says you're almost as useful as we are—" Lili said.

"And the *almost* is only because there's just one of you," Chiara clarified.

"And of course we can greet you properly—"

"Because if you've been yodelling *Tante* Martina—"

"You must be special—"

"But we can't try you out because—"

"You see, we're—"

"Off the menu," they said together.

"Stop that," Martina said, and Dequan turned gratefully to face her. She was smiling, so she must be delighted to have her previously-MIA nieces back at work.

He smiled back, pleased that she was pleased, but just a shade chagrined that their close café partnership was no longer exclusive.

To his surprise, Marina's beautiful face hardened, and she flicked her fingers at the young women. "Go and help Yannick, girls. I'll deal with you later."

"Yes, *Tante*," they said in chorus and they vanished towards the larder.

Martina's face softened again and she stepped up and put her arms around Dequan.

He hugged her back, surprised when she brought him in for a deep kiss. She broke it at last and pulled her lips back to murmur, "Let's go back to bed. I want to yodel with you right now."

Holding hands, they passed through to the chalet, and up

the stairs.

Dequan expected Martina to conjure off their clothing. Instead, she flung herself down on the Christmas coverlet just as she was, before lifting her skirts in a welter of petticoats.

Dequan scrambled out of his shorts and jocks and got down beside her. They rolled together and coupled with the practised joy of their days and nights together.

Martina gasped and said, "Oh, I was going to suck your balls first."

He thrust hard, trying to bury himself in her warmth. "Next time," he managed.

"Next time." She rolled them over and bore down before she flung back her head and yodelled.

That was quick, but —

He didn't get to finish the thought before his mind spun out.

When he recovered a little, he got onto his elbow and looked down at his lover. Her crown of hair was neat. Her clothing was laced and tied with ribbon bows. This was the café owner, not the *fräulein*. He kissed her tenderly.

"Greet you, Mistress Bless." He'd learned that was the correct styling for a full fay lady.

She opened her eyes. "What happened to *fräulein* or Martina?"

"You're dressed for work. That makes you a lady to be addressed with courtesy."

"Even when your cock is still inside me?"

"Especially then."

"Well then, my gentleman . . ." She kissed him again. "Did you see Master Peckerdale?"

"There was no one there, except for the geese."

"Oh?"

"They chased me home again. I think I've worked out why."

"Tell me." She pulled the lacing of her top loose, releasing her breasts.

Dequan kissed them in turn, bathing in the mocha scent. "Do you need to yodel again?"

She laughed. "Not yet. I just want to enjoy having you enjoy them. Tell me about the crazed geese."

"I think they really were attracted to the feather pin. Cèilidh said it was a come-to-be."

"But they didn't want it."

"No." He kissed her breasts again. "They didn't want it, but I think they wanted to get me to the luck it's supposed to bring. And you, with your *gentleman of the bedchamber* dreams and his flirting feather, must have seemed ideal . . ."

Martina snuggled against him and worked a hand down to play with his balls. "You think all that *Visigothing* was just them trying to bring us together?"

"Well . . . *ooh* . . ."

"Ooh?" she said playfully, as her hand persisted.

He swallowed. "They stopped once I was with you . . . and they don't mind me going out if I go with you . . . but they were there on the balcony for the great original yodel."

His lover shook with giggles. "*Gott im Himmel!* They watched us having one another and then, having achieved what they wanted, they marched off home!"

"It makes sense," he said.

"It makes no sense!"

"It makes as much sense as anything does in this daft town. And if you keep on playing down there, you'll have me blowing again and then you won't get to yodel."

"I like it when you blow. Relax and let go. No geese, no family, no work, no regrets, no comparisons, and no thoughts of tomorrow . . ."

He relaxed into her care and the build-up was going nicely along to the toe-curling stage when someone tapped on the door.

CHAPTER EIGHTEEN: GOOSE END

Martina, Patterdale, December Thirty-first

Martina loved it when her gentleman of the bedchamber, who was also her gooseman, and wholly her darling Dequan, put himself into her hands.

He was such a happy lover, often laughing, and always alert to any shift in her mood. She was working on him not only for his pleasure and hers, but to forget how angry she was with the twins and Yannick, who had greeted her when she arrived home from market.

She hadn't yet had a good explanation from them. She foresaw a family explosion once Nina and Florien found out the girls were home.

Nina was going to be furious.

Therefore, Martina was storing up pleasures against the coming storm.

She had got her gentleman blissed out and surging rhythmically in her hand when she heard the tap on the door.

Her hand stilled.

"Don't stop! Ooh . . ."

"Tante?"

She returned to her caress and quickly took her lover's mouth in a kiss to stifle his urgent moans as he spilled. "There, my darling, *meine Leibe . . .*"

"Tante? Dequan?"

Martina conjured her coverlet over Dequan and then sat up, jerking her bodice laces together.

"*Gott im Himmel!* What the devil do you *want*?" she snapped.

The door creaked open and two apologetic faces appeared. "Sorry, *Tante* Martina but there's a call —"

"It's for Dequan and the person says it's urgent."

Martina said curtly, "I can't imagine anything was urgent enough for you to come interrupting us."

Lili said, "I know. We've been awful, but we —"

"What about this call?" Martina asked.

She felt Dequan stirring and put a hand on his shoulder.

"It's for Dequan," Chiara said.

"You can let him come up for air. I should think he's back to his brain by now," Lili opined. She edged through the door and held out a phone at arm's length.

Martina didn't recognise it. "Where did you get that?"

Dequan fought his way out of the coverlet. He looked flushed, but he nodded to Lili and said politely, "Hello again, twin."

Chiara said from the door, "There's no need to be embarrassed, Dequan. I expect you don't want to talk right now, but this person —"

Martina conjured the phone into her hand, bringing a squeak from Lili. She glanced down at it and then said to Dequan, "I think this must be your phone. I'll leave you to deal with it while I deal with *them*." She got out of bed and stalked past Lili to the door. "Out," she said.

The twins clattered down the stairs with Martina in pursuit. She got them into the sitting room and glared at Yannick. He should have been in the larder. Instead, he was seated on the couch.

"Out. This is family business."

He glared back. "I am family." He turned his attention to the twins. He held out both arms, and the girls sat down on either side of him. "Okay, my lovelies?"

"Yes—"

"*Tante* Martina's just—"

"A bit—"

"Stop that." Martina pointed at Lili. "You. Tell me why you had Dequan's phone. You, Chiara, keep quiet. Yannick, go away."

Yannick stayed put.

Lili said, "After you and Dequan went upstairs to yodel one another, we saw Dequan had left his bag. We kept hearing texts and messages pinging."

Chiara said, "and then—"

Martina pointed at her younger niece. "Quiet." She pointed to Yannick. "Out."

Lili continued. "And then the phone rang. It kept on ringing and ringing and we thought it must be important."

"So—"

"Hush," Martina said.

"Hush yourself." Yannick glowered at her. "Stop bullying my wives."

"Your—*Gott im Himmel! Großer Gott im Himmel*! Nina is going to *kill* me!"

Yannick said, "I answered the phone. The person wanted to speak to Dequan Qin right now. She said it was urgent. That's why my lovelies brought the phone to you. We didn't think you'd want me in there."

Martina sighed. That was the most connected words Yannick had said to her in three years.

She was about to demand further clarification when Dequan came into the sitting room. He had resumed his clothing, and he looked distressed.

He held out his arms to Martina.

She went to him immediately. "What, *mein Liebe*?"

He held her tightly. "It's the V-S driver. She's here. She's been messaging for three hours but my phone was in the B&B

and it wasn't working."

Martina stared at him numbly. "V-S. Already?"

She'd known he was on a holiday, but they'd never discussed the length of his stay.

"I forgot. I plain put it out of my mind. Martina . . . I tried to put her off, but she says she'll lose her job if I don't come now. She's contracted to return me to my pick-up point today."

His arms slackened. "I have to go, but I'll call you. I promise."

Martina opened her mouth to say something. A sob came out.

She was vaguely aware of Yannick getting up from between the twins. He didn't do emotions, so he must be fleeing the scene.

Dequan hugged her fiercely. "Martina . . ."

They stood clasped together.

Outside in the street, a loud honking sounded.

Those geese.

She tried to believe it, but she knew it was a car horn. That driver was getting impatient.

"I have to go," Dequan said.

"Yes." Martina stepped back and then collapsed onto the couch between the twins. They put their arms around her, animosity forgotten.

The door closed quietly behind her darling gooseman.

She strained her ears to hear the car driving away, but all she could hear was a dull thudding in her brain.

The door opened again and she looked up, blurry-eyed, into Yannick's most formidable frown. "*Tante* Martina, get cracking."

"What?" She gaped at him.

"Move. I just spent my holiday bonus on a Vouch-Safe voucher for you and talked the driver into servicing it now instead of waiting for a vacancy. Go." He jerked his head.

Martina said, "The café—"

"We'll look after that," Lili said.

"We'll look after everything," Chiara added.

"Get going. There are six geese a laying out there honking the place down," Yannick said.

Martina conjured a facecloth and then, on an afterthought, she conjured the feathers from the drawer in her bedchamber.

She and Dequan were going to need them.

ABOUT THE AUTHOR

Lark Westerly lives on the island state of Tasmania.

One of her favourite occupations is weaving stories about the mix of fairy and human characters in the *Fairy in the Bed, Red Cat, Tamzin,* and *Pixie Grip* series.

To find out more about the *Fairy in the Bed* world, visit Lark virtually at https://larksinger.weebly.com

www.ingramcontent.com/pod-product-compliance
Lightning Source LLC
Chambersburg PA
CBHW060644130626
46555CB00002B/947